FREE THERAPY

FREE THERAPY

Stories

REBECCA IVORY

JONATHAN CAPE
LONDON

1 3 5 7 9 10 8 6 4 2

Jonathan Cape, an imprint of Vintage, is part of the Penguin Random House group of companies whose addresses can be found at global.penguinrandomhouse.com

First published by Jonathan Cape in 2024

penguin.co.uk/vintage

Typeset in 14/16.55pt Perpetua Std by Jouve (UK), Milton Keynes
Printed and bound in Great Britain by Clays Ltd, Elcograf S.p.A.

The authorised representative in the EEA is Penguin Random House Ireland, Morrison Chambers, 32 Nassau Street, Dublin D02 YH68

A CIP catalogue record for this book is available from the British Library

HB ISBN 9781787334687
TPB ISBN 9781787334694

Penguin Random House is committed to a sustainable future for our business, our readers and our planet. This book is made from Forest Stewardship Council® certified paper.

It's called, my mother might have said, an inner life: the one thing nobody can take away from you.

—Elizabeth McCracken, *The Hero of This Book*

———

For my family

Contents

Push and Pull

At fifteen, I couldn't fit into my clothes anymore. Shorts I had worn the previous summer could not be zipped up, t-shirts strained across my chest and arms. My breasts had grown larger — suddenly and painfully. I imagined myself to be too broad in the back and graceless in my movements. There was a new smell that came from between my legs when I sat down, of rust and bread. I spent much of that summer with my friend Tara, who had always been slightly larger than me. My self-disgust triggered in her a new awareness, and she was prompted to examine the spread of her own thighs and stomach, to compare the width of her hips with the circumference of her waist. We agreed that our developing femininity was excessive, that an overall reduction might help to counteract it. We experimented with a diet of popcorn and chicken and fruit and salted crackers. We twisted and craned in front of bedroom mirrors, to confirm how pale and expansive and odd our bodies appeared to other people and how best to conceal this. We positioned bra straps and waistbands carefully to prevent our flesh from bulging over. We informed one another when we sat or stood or walked in an unflattering way. This mutual criticism couldn't be taken back simply because of hurt feelings; that would have been dishonest. Our behaviour was competitive and collaborative, and the mutual appraisal was essential for any improvement. This process was casual and cruel and intimate, and I thought about it all the time.

After six weeks, I had lost three pounds and Tara had lost almost six. Mostly, it was noticeable only around her face. When Tara stopped holding her breath, her stomach still hung over the waistband of her underwear and so did mine. Our upper arms remained pimply and red and soft. Even still, her progress unnerved me, given that my own was much slower. Tara remarked on our similarities, which she found amusing. Privately, I was offended. I had assumed I would always look better than she did. My disgust for the both of us deepened. I expressed anger towards my body in ways that embarrassed me: alone in my room, I cried in frustration while tugging and scratching violently at my flesh. If I experienced hunger pains, I started to pound at my stomach with my fist, as if the hunger would defer to violence. Once I calmed down, I experienced a cold and crystallised shame: as well as being disgusting, I was hateful and bizarre.

In August, Tara was due to leave Ireland for a three-week retreat to Spain with her family. Her parents were deeply religious, and the purpose of the trip was to undertake a pilgrimage all together. Before her departure she was agitated; it would be much harder to maintain the same level of control at mealtimes, she'd have to eat whatever her family ate.

'There will be so much walking every day, you'll just burn off everything you eat,' I said casually. 'I'll probably end up losing all my motivation while you're away too. We can start fresh when you're back.' This was a lie. I planned to be even more vigilant in her absence. I hoped to convince her that she could safely give in to complacency. Tara only rolled her eyes in response as she packed her suitcase, and I could not tell if she believed me.

Once she left, I began to exercise intensely, in an attempt to create an acceptable gap between us once more. I pedalled my mother's stationary bike every evening and ran loops around the village early in the mornings so people wouldn't see me. I restricted what I ate even further, spitting chewed-up food into a napkin. Ten days into Tara's trip away, I received a postcard from Cadíz, a place I had never heard of. She wrote only two lines: 'Having a good time but missing you. See you when I get back :)'

After two weeks, I had lost another seven pounds, which was less than I'd expected. I didn't grow downy hair or develop poor circulation, but I was cold and undeniably smaller. My body did not look good naked; I still considered it pale and blemished and misshapen. But this didn't matter to me because I was closer to achieving the androgynous aesthetic I felt most comfortable with. In moments when I felt my commitment wavering, I imagined that Tara would return home as her previous self, after three weeks of eating greasy, indulgent food. The idea of this appealed to me more than the optics of weight loss.

At that time, there was also the matter of my mother, a retired musician who still taught students from our home. She could no longer perform professionally due to arthritis in her hands and wrists. We both paid little attention to housework and mealtimes, and she spent most of her free hours reading at the kitchen table. Because she was often in pain, she was often irritable. Our house was a cramped bungalow and from my bedroom down the hallway, I heard her at night muttering to herself, cursing the pain, the broken appliances, the money. I heard splashing liquids and slamming glasses and bitter talk that grew more confused and accusatory. Other than this, the house was quiet.

Tara arrived home the last weekend in August. We were due to start third year the following Monday. We planned to meet on Sunday afternoon at my house. We usually hung around hers, but she wanted a break from her parents and younger brothers after three weeks together. I was edgy and restless all morning for two reasons. I was conscious that my mother would be home and that she might find our teenage chatter and excitement obnoxious and agitating. She didn't like Tara, who was unaware of this. I was also anxious about how Tara might react to my changed body. Even my mother, who was mostly detached from anything beyond the provision of shelter and basic nourishment, watched me over the pages of her book and remarked that I should be careful: skinny people get sick more frequently than larger ones. Now that I was faced with seeing Tara again, my sudden weight loss felt like a betrayal rather than a triumph.

On Sunday morning, I paced the house, pausing to

check my reflection, wishing that I could look fuller again. At two o'clock, I heard Tara's mother's car pull up and I rushed to open the door. There was immediate excitement from the two of us and she wrapped her arms around my neck for a hug. My smile kept contracting and wobbling. She shouted hello to my mother who was sat quietly in the kitchen, pretending not to hear her. I carried on, leading us both towards my room, where Tara pulled herself onto my bed, sitting cross-legged. I was acutely aware of how I moved my body and could not let my hands lie still. I settled for leaning on the windowsill and folding my arms over my chest.

'Are you happy to be home?' I asked her, my voice high-pitched.

'You look very thin,' she replied quickly, ignoring the question. Her voice was cheerful in a way I thought might be sarcastic.

I knew I couldn't return this compliment because, as I had expected, she had put back on any weight she had lost. I feared that saying otherwise might provoke explicit anger. She tilted her head to the side and cocked her jaw, considering my appearance. 'You look good, but you're still quite spotty,' she said, before adjusting the pillows and lying back. 'Your forehead is *so* shiny.'

Throughout the day, Tara ate more than I did. She kept requesting snacks from the kitchen. I brought her rice cakes, which she refused, asking for biscuits instead. She quickly ate five in a row, talking with her mouth full and spraying wet crumbs onto my duvet. I had green tea. We went to the newsagent's, where she bought coke and crisps and chocolate, things we would have eaten together earlier that year. Rather than feeling disgusted with Tara's indulgence, I felt guilty for not joining in. When her mother arrived to pick her up at six o'clock, I was relieved to see her go.

*

That September, we resumed a school-time friendship with two other girls, Erica and Maria. We had very little in common but had all attended the same primary school and so they seemed like natural allies when we started secondary school. Tara and I were interested in music and art. Erica considered all creative pursuits to be worthless and embarrassing. This was a belief instilled in her by her parents, who helped wealthy people manage their money. Over the summer, Erica's acne had cleared up, and her braces had been removed. She returned to school with a boyfriend – a popular fourth-year student who lacked any sense of humour. We formed an odd little group with his friends during lunch, and although we rarely spoke to each other, we gradually decided who ought to pair off. Maria ended up with a very stupid but gentle boy. I had been assigned to a boy named Luke, who was so conventionally attractive that it made me feel apprehensive about eye contact and being alone with him. Tara showed no interest in any of these boys. In return, they quietly mocked her bad breath and constant absent-minded singing and humming.

Within the first couple weeks of school, I could already tell that Maria and Erica were losing patience with Tara. She could be both volatile and remote, erupting with goofy, unbidden laughter only to abruptly stop and stare blankly at any boy attempting to engage her, even when they were trying to be friendly. In these moments, I felt wholly responsible for her and looked at my shoes or turned away, not wanting to witness the ways in which she alienated herself.

'She needs to stop following us around. She's *embarrassing* us,' Erica told me in early October.

'She's embarrassing herself,' Maria added, her face wilting with pity.

Instead of insisting that Tara be included and accepted, I began to maintain my own friendship with her separately. I never explained to her what Erica had said and watched with growing anxiety as she trailed along behind us, becoming more and more uncertain of her peripheral position in our foursome. I kept myself busy talking to Erica and Maria and lingering near the boys, aware of how rarely anyone acknowledged Tara. I felt guilty and wished she would just go away.

When Tara and I were alone, I hoped we might be able to pretend it wasn't happening. Unsurprisingly, she was hurt by my disloyalty, my refusal to admit we were freezing her out. She criticised my fawning, my efforts to impress Luke and his friends. I laughed at Luke's jokes, which were often regurgitated from Will Ferrell movies. They weren't funny and I was mortified that Tara should draw attention to my pandering. She scolded me for skipping lunch, telling me I looked awful, that maybe I'd lost some weight but now my hair was dull and my skin too pale. I was nervous to be alone with her but didn't have the courage to cut her off completely. Our relationship started to feel more and more like stumbling and skidding down a hill of thorns; I avoided impact where possible but couldn't control our trajectory.

Throughout the winter, I continued to eat very little. I learned how to be subtle and precise when applying make-up and styling my hair. This was time-consuming, and I lost interest in reading and music and anything else outside of myself. Erica gave Luke my number and we texted each other constantly. I kept chewing and spitting out my food and exercising at five o'clock in the morning. Rather than feeling weak or depleted, I took deep satisfaction in this erasure of my body and mind. It was not the polished exterior that I valued, so much as the secrecy of my discipline. There was a private and remote space within myself, an interior room I could visit to feel superior and resilient. At this point, I felt so alone in my life that such delusions were easy to believe.

I still spent my Friday nights with Tara to keep her happy. The tension between us could be temporarily relieved during our sleepovers at her house, where I slipped quietly into a chaotic, messy and happy sort of atmosphere. She lived on a dairy farm. Tara's mother was an elegant woman whose refinement surprised me because her house was so untidy. I found Tara's older brother very attractive. Tara regarded him with such reverence and admiration that I sometimes wondered if she did too. On the other hand, Tara's stepfather, Jack, made me feel uneasy. He owned the farm and was at least ten years older than Tara's mother. He was short and compact, with thick dark hair on his head, hands and arms. He was so playful and inquisitive; he could easily embarrass me by listening intently when I spoke, by expecting me to contribute honestly to adult conversations. To counter this, I developed a heightened sense of self-consciousness around him. It was uncomfortable and tiring, like wearing a flattering but constrictive dress.

Tara and I had our last sleepover together in December. Her mother went to bed early, as she usually did. Her older brother was out with friends. The two younger children fell asleep on the couch in front of the television and were coaxed upstairs by Tara and me. The youngest one circled his arms around my torso, declaring he wanted me to sleep in his bed. I smiled with a benevolence that I didn't truly feel. Tara shooed him away and by eleven o'clock, it was just us and Jack. He offered us small, brown bottles of beer, which tasted like medicine. Their television showed an American news show. Jack shushed us every so often in order to hear what the news anchor had said. He condemned American politicians I had never heard of, saying that things weren't much better here. Jack believed quite seriously that all politicians, conservative and liberal, were inherently evil, as were many celebrities. His arguments were flimsy and obstinate in their failure to acknowledge nuance or complexity. I was surprised by how earnest and gullible he seemed, and I pitied him for it. After about half an hour, our bottles were empty, and Jack pulled himself out of his chair to get another. Identifying a natural break in his monologue, Tara suggested we go to bed now too.

'Deserting me once you've had your drinks, that's lousy!' Jack objected. He was standing, shaking his head.

I was embarrassed and, in my uncertainty, I sat back down on the couch, my cheeks burning. Tara protested but also joined me. Jack laughed triumphantly and walked towards the kitchen.

'Well, you needn't think I'll be giving you anymore, either way,' he said, carrying one bottle for himself back to the couch.

He sat down and searched for the remote before retrieving it from under a cushion and muting the television. He lifted an index finger and resumed his stream of complaints about the destruction of community, the degradation of traditional values and, ultimately, the fading role of religion in modern life. His hands moved in circular motions before his face as he spoke. The only pauses were for him to incline his head slightly to identify the next words. We were expected to wait patiently. I was certain that if we had interrupted, we would have been ignored. The outdoor sensor lamps were activated intermittently and cast a cold column of light through the dark room. When he eventually concluded, his expression was one of serious reflection. Perhaps he was waiting for my response, but I didn't know what I ought to say. Tara tore intently at her fingernails with her teeth, spitting them to the ground once removed.

After a moment, Jack turned to regard me with a broad smile.

'I have to say, Sarah, you're very good with the children. An unusual talent for an only child. You'd be an excellent mother.'

I looked at Tara, who rolled her eyes but otherwise seemed unconcerned.

'Have you thought about whether you want children yet?' he asked me, softly.

'Stop Jack, that's such a weird thing to say,' Tara intercepted, before turning to me. 'You don't need to answer that.'

'What?' he asked, feigning innocence. 'You don't mind, do you?' He shifted his torso to me and, without looking at Tara, held a palm up to instruct her to be quiet. 'You're very sweet to them. That's all I meant.'

I smiled to let him know I understood, and he winked at me.

'You should come and see the new calves with their mothers.' He pointed his beer bottle at me before taking a large mouthful and swallowing. 'They're only a few days old.'

'That might be nice.' I looked to Tara, hoping she might assert herself once more in this exchange. She only looked dully back at my stupid, smiling face.

'Well, come on, let's get you some boots then.' Jack stood up and walked to the patio door, where there was a mess of runners and boots.

'What? You want to go right now?' I asked.

He turned and threw a pair of boots caked in muck at my feet. 'Yeah, come on. Don't worry, I'll protect you,' he said, squeezing my shoulder briefly.

'No, Jack,' Tara said wearily. 'It's too dark and cold.'

He sat back down to lace up his own boots. 'I have a torch,' he said, yanking the laces tight. 'Anyway, you don't have to come if you don't want to, Tara.'

I searched both Jack and Tara's faces, waiting for

instructions. Jack laughed and hurried out to the hall to get two coats. Tara sat up and tucked her legs beneath her, watching him leave the sitting room.

'This is ridiculous,' she said. 'Why are you entertaining him?'

I didn't know the answer to her question. I wasn't sure who held the power in this situation, but I wanted him to like me, to like looking at me. I don't think he knew I was aware of his interest in me, that I could notice his gaze in my peripheral vision. I suspect he preferred the idea of my being oblivious.

'Right,' Jack said, returning to sitting room. 'Let's go.'

He threw a coat onto my lap, and I pulled it on, feeling stiff.

'You're not seriously going, are you?' Tara said, as I stood to join Jack at the door.

I ignored her and followed Jack in the oversized boots across the grass. I looked back at the house, expecting Tara to rush out after us. Instead, she stood at the patio door with her arms crossed, watching.

We reached the shed within a few minutes, his torch offering a blurred and failing light. He pulled his hat down over his ears and slid the steel door open. The torch flickered along the length of the wall as he searched for the light switch. He pressed it and the space inside illuminated gradually. The shed was long and narrow, and the cows were penned in to one side. The walls were damp, the floor was brown and red. The cows shifted and moved away from us, bobbing their heads and shooting strings of mucus from their nostrils with each exhaling breath. At the very end of the shed was a separate pen with two cows and their calves, lying on a pile of wet straw. Their coats were still damp and shiny and curling around their ears. They trembled as their mothers sniffed and licked their heads. I leaned against the gate and spoke to them in a babyish voice, exaggerating my excitement because I hoped to please Jack. They stood up unsteadily, disturbed by our visit. Wet and matted straw clung to their backsides, and their movement carried with it the smell of blood and shit. Jack stood right behind me, gripping the top of the gate. I could feel him breathing heavily on my neck, but I pretended to be unaffected by this. After a moment or two, I had run out of things to say about the calves and turned around, expecting him to make space, but he stayed standing there, and when my hip brushed his leg there was something so nakedly adamant and curious in his expression that it frightened me. He watched me and smiled with his mouth open, the way you might while waiting for a joke to be told. When I couldn't find the next thing to say, the next thing to do, he let go of the gate and coughed and spat on the ground. He told me he wanted to check in on the mothers while we were here, and I stood waiting with my sleeves pulled over my hands. Water had seeped into the boots, and so my feet were wet. In the pen, he handled the mothers' stomachs and backsides roughly and cursed them for protesting. I felt anxious in case one should charge and crush him and I would have to run back to the house and find help, but they only resigned themselves to the examination. Even from where I stood, I could see their still-bloody openings. Jack was unnecessarily harsh and thorough in his probing and prodding, and even as a teenager I could recognise his impermissible anger, the performance required of him to hide it.

We didn't speak on the way back to the house. As soon as we returned, Tara jumped off the couch and announced we were going to bed. I pulled the boots off and apologised for getting mud on the floor.

'Don't worry about it,' Tara said impatiently.

'Can I get a kiss goodnight, Tara?' Jack held his arms out expectantly, his good mood almost completely restored.

'Good night,' she said sternly, as she walked past him and towards the foot of the stairs.

'Ah, now, what's this? You'll give me a kiss, won't you, Sarah?' He leaned forwards, tilting his cheek towards me.

I pecked his cheek and turned to see Tara still standing at the stairs, her face tense and still.

I lay on my side on the bottom bunk with Tara above me. It wasn't unusual for us to fall asleep in the same bed, but that night she climbed the ladder to the top bunk silently.

'Tara, I'm sorry, I didn't mean to upset you,' I whispered.

She only sighed impatiently. Eventually her breathing became deep and regular and I sensed she had fallen asleep. I could not sleep. I was nervous that Tara would not speak to me other than to tell me directly all the ways that I had failed as a friend, failures I could not deny. I was disturbed too by my experience with Jack in the shed. Every time I thought about it, my face flushed with fresh embarrassment and fear. I couldn't tell how responsible I was for what had happened. And yet I was excited by the certainty that Jack desired me. My mind wandered to images of Jack examining my body, running his hands along my cold limbs and down my navel and over my hip bones and being turned on by how young and thin I was. I thought about the wiry hair on his coarse hands, which would cup my crotch before slipping inside. It was disgusting and desirable and these two things weren't necessarily in opposition to one another. I pictured Tara and Erica and Maria finding out what Jack and I had done. Initially, the idea of this revelation horrified me, but as the fantasy evolved my friends took an active role, bearing witness to the imagined intimacies, and this became something I wanted. I replayed the images on a loop, compelled to see how much I could fabricate before fear and revulsion and instinct superseded this desire and pushed me away again.

The following morning, Tara gave me cereal with milk from their farm, which made me sick as it was unpasteurised. I spent the rest of the morning doubled over with cramps in her bed. Her little brother brought me toys and laid them out in a semi-circle around the bed like small gifts. He stood beside the toys poking my face.

'Yuck. Your skin is so greasy. And you have so many little red spots,' he said.

I asked him to go get Tara.

'How are you feeling?' she asked flatly, tugging a brush through her wet hair.

'Awful. Do you think your mam could drive me home?'

'Fine. Oh, be careful getting out of bed,' she said, pointing to the arrangement of toys on the floor. 'He likes to leave little soldiers and Lego on the ground like that, so you'll stand on them and hurt your feet.'

I slept much better in my own bed. I woke in the late afternoon feeling well enough to exercise, and then threw my clothes into the washing machine to get rid of the smell of Tara's house and their animals. I showered and spent the evening in my room, aware of how quiet my home was, how nice it was to be left alone.

On Monday, I met Maria and Erica at our lockers before a tutorial. Tara wasn't in yet; she always arrived minutes before the bell rang.

'How was your *sleepover*?' Erica asked. Her voice was whiny. She was mocking me.

'It was fine, boring really,' I said. It's what I always said.

'Well, you must enjoy them. You go every week,' Maria said.

Erica was texting now, distracted.

'I'd feel bad if I didn't,' I said defensively. 'Anyway, I don't think I'll go again.'

Erica looked up with renewed interest. 'Why? What happened?'

Normally, I wouldn't say anything that might implicate Tara and cause a further rift. This now struck me as pointless. I didn't want to be her friend any longer. I had been waiting for a reason to bring things to an end, and here it was.

'Tara's stepfather is so creepy,' I said, leaning in to give the details to Erica and Maria. Their eager reaction only encouraged me, and by the time I had finished the story, the good-night kiss was forcibly applied and wet. I could have carried on talking about it, adding further embellishment, exaggerating the ways in which he touched me, but I stopped once I saw Tara approach as the bell rang.

'Hi Tara,' Erica said brightly.

Maria laughed nervously and Tara's face fell.

'What's going on?' Tara asked.

'Nothing. Maria's just hyper,' I said. 'I have a tutorial, so I'll see you later.'

I spent the rest of the day trying to convince myself I had done nothing wrong. I replayed the conversation with Erica and Maria, sorting out the truth from the lies, wondering to what extent Erica would distort my already-false claims and how long it would be before the story made its way around the school. As for Tara, I was deliberately distant with her during our art class, but my confidence faltered when I saw how much it bewildered her. Part of me had hoped she might still be angry. At least then it would have been a mutual falling out. But she was good humoured and even managed to laugh when Luke's friends lifted the back of her skirt with a stick during the walk between classes. I felt a mounting anxiety all morning, imagining her reaction when she found out what I had said. Rumours and suspicions were circulating around her and she had no idea. Despite wanting rid of Tara, I hated myself for lying, not just because I had been cruel but because I was careless and clumsy in telling Erica, of all people, who could not be trusted to handle this information sensibly or subtly, to smear Tara's reputation while preserving mine. Until that point, I hadn't considered myself as a person with such foolish tendencies.

Tara didn't approach me until after the final bell. I knew from her urgent, determined expression that she had heard about what I said. I found that I was relieved.

'Have you been telling people that Jack is a pervert?'

Even the use of the word, how crude and exaggerated it seemed, mortified me.

'Who told you that?' I asked, stupidly.

'Erica's been telling everyone that he forced you to kiss him. What did you say to her?' Her voice broke and I wanted to pull her to me, to take her outside and explain.

'I was there for the whole thing,' she continued. 'You didn't have to kiss him goodnight. I didn't kiss him. No one forced you.' She stepped closer to me. 'Why did you say that?'

Things probably could have been salvaged had I responded differently. But I find apologies cumbersome and draining. I prefer to bear down and ride it out. Besides, it would have been too awful to admit I had lied, too shameful.

'Well, in fairness, Tara, I did feel forced into it.' I had hoped to be certain, but the words came haltingly. 'He knew I was uncomfortable. The whole night was weird.'

I stared at the padlock on my locker, running my finger over its ridges to comfort myself. This will be over soon, I thought.

'Oh, come on Sarah, you loved it,' she said evenly. 'You're desperate for attention. That's the only reason you never eat.'

Conversations around us trailed off as people waited to see what would happen next.

'You'd *love* it if someone tried to molest you, for the sympathy if nothing else,' Tara said.

There was a flicker of violence inside my throat, something provoked by her speaking so directly, some fear that she was right. With surprising clarity, it occurred to me that Tara was more intelligent than I was.

'Just leave me alone, Tara. Go fuck off back to your paedophile stepdad.' I pushed past, shouldering her as I went. She pushed me in return, and I stumbled from the force of it, but hurried away, too frightened to look back.

Obviously, it was awful. Once our parents found out, the school had to get involved. It was so embarrassing: I had to admit it wasn't true or else they'd rope social services into the situation and then there would have to be a proper investigation. They didn't force me to apologise, but I did see Tara's stepfather leaving the administration office after a meeting with the principal. I was due to go in afterwards with my mother. He didn't even seem angry. Tara and her mother hurried past us, but Jack slowed his pace and gave me a brief, tight smile. He could afford to be nice to me, given I was a proven liar. I thought at the time that he might have even felt sorry for me. I wondered if he felt he had overestimated me, that I had mishandled something that deserved care and discretion and maturity and that, as a result, I had disappointed him. I was probably wrong; he probably thought nothing about me and hardly remembered the interactions between us. I smiled at his shoes as he walked by with his hands in his pockets.

By this stage, Erica had started making up stories about me. Rumours circulated that I had tried to seduce Jack, that we had had sex and that I was pregnant. I didn't care because I now spent all of my time with Luke, who didn't seem to mind either way. I was completely obsessed with him. While I still ate very little, my attempts to win Luke's approval and affection replaced weight loss as my ultimate objective in life. We spent three years fighting and having sex and promising not to fight again and he was the only thing I could think about until I went to college and cheated on him with the first boy who showed an interest in me.

When I was twenty-two, my mother told me that Tara's mother had left Jack. She and my mother had started attending the same aqua aerobics class, an activity my mother found relieved some of her stiffness.

'That *predator*,' as my mother insisted on calling him, 'ran the business into the ground. They had to sell up, and now she's stuck in a tiny flat with the youngest child while he's gone to live with his brother up North.'

In recent years, my mother had stopped drinking, and this only made her mood worse. Her caustic remarks about Jack made my skin crawl, and I couldn't fully understand why.

'I don't think you should be sharing those details, Mam. She might have told you in confidence,' I said.

'What would you know about it?' she snapped, fixing me with a narrow and critical look.

I left it there. I lacked the courage needed to challenge her. My mother's scorn left me with an impotent, exaggerated sort of anger, a kind that made me slam doors and hold a pillow to my mouth and scream.

Ten years later, I had a boyfriend who hit me four times and often threatened to wring my neck. I found myself squaring back up to him during these furious moments, to make things equal. We were ridiculous. He was a tall and grey man from Finland. An academic. He was ugly and sexy at the same time, which is what I like. Eventually, he landed me in hospital. We were in the garden, arguing. He pushed too hard, and I knew it was an accident on his part. Afterwards, his hands were shaking so badly he could hardly hang on to the steering wheel when he drove me to A&E. I was remarkably calm and watched him while pressing a wet face cloth to my bloody forehead. He held his fingertips to his mouth and would let out a groan of despair every time he looked at me. I had to suppress the urge to laugh. He was afraid he'd get in trouble. His fear was disgusting to me. What had he expected?

Before all that, we did stupid, incongruent things, like go to galleries and museums and bookshops together. Once, he took me to see a play in Dublin. In the dark theatre, he held my knee still. The stage was bare. The play relied heavily on monologues. Most of the actors played multiple characters. Almost halfway through, I realised that one of the actors on stage was Tara. Even as an adult, I found myself appraising her body, which had of course changed in the intervening years. She had taken on a more athletic shape, and I experienced a fleeting envy. She was dressed in black and played three different characters but, essentially, they were all the same. She didn't strike me as particularly talented, but I got a kick out of watching her. I had been working in human resources for three years and had never pursued anything that I could maintain a meaningful interest in.

Afterwards, in the car on the way home, I told my boyfriend that I had gone to school with one of the actors and that I had done something awful to her. He was driving through an awkward junction and didn't respond right away. Then he shrugged, said he didn't know which actor I was talking about. I tried to describe her, to help him remember. I kept describing her. Frustrated now, he said he had no idea who I was talking about. Don't be so obsessive, he told me, cutting a hand through the air, what does it matter anyway? Could I really think he cared about something that happened between two stupid teenagers? Things escalated from there: shouting, screaming, a hassle for us out of nowhere, a problem I didn't predict or ask for.

And in moments like these, I return to my private and remote place, that old interior room situated somewhere behind my eyes. There was a time when I believed I could derive strength from this isolation, that it made me superior, a more compelling person, someone that the right kind of people were drawn to at a party. But there's no party in this room, and the people in my imagination who were delayed have finally called to cancel altogether, telling me I ought to just invite the people I already know instead, the other women like me. This strikes me as worse than having to sit alone in the room, so I stay put in my dull little space, decorated with dated artefacts of diminishing accomplishments from another era.

Free Therapy

Richie was upset with me because I let a woman skip us in the queue at the supermarket. Letting her go first was such an automatic impulse to me that, at first, I didn't even recognise his sudden reticence as anger. Too nervous to let the silence take centre stage, I rambled on, hoping it would pass. Back in my apartment, hailstones fell steadily against the window. Inside, I began to tentatively tug at his frustration, which upon being unfurled, could not be rewound and tidily tucked away in the same fashion.

'It's just, you're so passive,' he complained. 'How will you get any respect in life when you let everyone walk all over you?'

'She was *old*, Richie,' I said. 'Would you rather I tell her to get back to the end of the line?'

'Why do you need me to tell you the right thing to do?' he asked, his voice suddenly aloof and condescending. 'If you're truly happy with your actions, you shouldn't need me to approve of them.'

'Oh, I thought you *liked* telling me what to do,' I said

quietly, turning away and sliding tinned tomatoes onto the shelf, 'at least when we're having sex, anyway.'

I liked him more than he liked me, and this was the only leverage I had, the ability to shame his private desires. He liked for me to lie back on the bed while he knelt above me, calling me names, turning my face one way, my body the other. I knew this was an opaque and embarrassing topic for him, something I could prod slightly and still elicit a reaction.

'Oh my God,' he groaned. His neck grew red at the collar. 'Your immaturity is incredible, really. We're not our*selves* in those moments. I can want different things from you, at different times.'

It was getting dark outside. We hadn't turned on the lights or heating yet, so the kitchen grew dim and cold. In the shopping bag remained several apples and a bottle of dish soap.

'It's just too much of a responsibility, having to tip-toe around your low self-esteem,' he said eventually, taking long, slow steps from the fridge to the sink and tugging at the hem of his shirt. I stood in the doorway watching him.

'And it's not just today, it's been niggling me all along. What is it you even want out of life?' he demanded.

We'd had this conversation several times, in one way or another. It would start off with some asinine remark and devolve into paranoia and crisis, the subtext being that I was derailing his focus and luring him into mediocrity.

Richie worked as a salesman in fintech and was obsessed with productivity and career progression. Meanwhile, I'd have liked a little more money and also for him to agree to be my boyfriend, which after four months he still had yet to do. I knew he'd consider my desires too simple, so I rarely talked about what I wanted. It was a convenient arrangement because for his part, he hadn't asked, until now.

'See! See what I mean!' He clicked his fingers when it was clear I couldn't respond. 'These are things you need to know about yourself, Alison!'

*

'You need to come to my women's group,' Martha said, as she dried herself off in the gym changing room.

'Yes, self-improvement,' I said, glumly. 'Richie would love that idea.'

In the immediate aftermath, I'd been stunned and embarrassed. It was like singing a duet, only for the other person to abruptly fall quiet, so that you're forced to hear how your voice really sounds to everyone else. In this solo, you realise, Wait, I'm talentless, completely tone deaf. Now, two months later, I still missed him.

'It's not just that I miss *him,*' I told her. 'I feel completely inadequate now, as if I wasn't good enough for him.'

'You felt that way already, that's why you ended up with Richie in the first place,' she said.

I threw her an indignant look, to hide how much this truth stung me.

'Seriously, that's why you need this group,' she said.

I knew Martha through the gym. She was thirty-two and a recovered bulimic, something she overcame through CrossFit and talking therapy. By the time I met her, she was a midwifery student who used tea tree oil as perfume.

She was six years older than me, and in the wake of my break-up, I found myself trailing along behind her, going with her when she ran errands and attended appointments. She was busy and radiated an emotional stability I envied. Sometimes, I imagined her as the kind of woman Richie pined after, a woman who knew her path and pursued it with or without him. I found the idea painful and compelling. It was perhaps for this reason that I agreed to try Martha's group, to see if it could help illuminate my own purpose, one I would stick to, unwavering, unaffected by matters of the heart.

*

The group could be found in a single-storey building, situated between a curtain manufacturer and a wholesale stationery distributor. Attendance was free of charge. It was a registered charity and members could offer donations as frequently as they liked or not at all. I was a little thrown by the set-up, having expected something like a yoga or meditation class, with affirmations and breathing exercises, attended by young full-time mothers and self-obsessed urban professionals. The room smelt damp and the women were badly dressed, the atmosphere tense. I felt that attending had been a mistake.

The first woman in the circle to speak was Johanna. She had a bare face with watery eyes and a tremulous voice. She provided full-time care to her elderly mother and needed a place where she could vent her anger, free of judgement.

'I have two sisters, but they're no help,' she rolled her eyes bitterly, 'as one lives abroad and the other has *four* children.'

The violence that rippled across her face as she spoke frightened me. She was so honestly disappointed with her life and obligations that it served to ward off any empty, meaningless words of optimism or comfort. Reassurance would have been a lie, an unhelpful reflex that had more to do with our discomfort than her situation.

The next woman, Dina, wore a sleeveless aquamarine top and had voluminous, jet-black hair. Her husband was an alcoholic. Their two sons idolised him and had very little time for her. Both sons had been charged with drink driving on different occasions. She'd felt completely alone, she explained, before finding this group. While she spoke, one of her bra straps kept slipping off her shoulder.

'And before you even ask,' she said wearily, tugging at the strap, 'leaving is impossible because my husband has all the money.'

The youngest woman, Shauna, was nineteen and had joined only six weeks before me. She spoke very little in her introduction and even still she was reduced to tears. Her problems struck me as abstract and difficult to grasp. I wondered how she had found *this* place. It was obvious that she was deeply depressed and perhaps beyond the help of the group, in need instead of medical care.

Then there was Josephine, our emphatic French group facilitator. She ran through her list of various, if vague, qualifications. Somehow, this managed to make her seem less credible, as if her tendency to jump from one field to the next cast doubt on her commitment and stability. But she struck me almost immediately as a beautiful and commanding presence.

When Josephine invited me to speak a little bit about my own experience, I began to feel nervous, certain my complaint was petty compared with those of the rest of the group.

'I broke up with my boyfriend, recently,' I nodded, before correcting myself. 'Actually, he wasn't really my boyfriend, I just hoped he would be.'

'He must have led you on, then, surely,' Dina offered kindly.

I shook my head. 'No. He'd been clear from the beginning that he didn't want anything serious, that it would be too distracting for him. I thought maybe he'd change his mind, but of course that wasn't the case.'

'And why is it you've been so affected by this, if it was just casual, as you say?' Josephine asked.

'I'm not sure,' I replied. 'It was very hot and cold. I just got too attached.'

'I see,' she nodded. 'Do you think this is a pattern? Your perception of a relationship not matching the reality?'

I paused, shrugging at the question. Before meeting Richie, I had found myself infatuated with my cousin's boyfriend. Unwisely, I acted on this impulse, only to find the feeling was unrequited, leaving me with the same disappointment and shame I was currently experiencing.

Noticing my hesitation, an amused expression crossed Josephine's face. 'Okay, we'll leave that for now. What was it that drew you to Richie in the first place?'

Again, I had to take time to consider this question. I liked that he was short and dark, thin as a jockey. He was also very funny on Twitter, with almost eight thousand followers. Mostly though, I was drawn in by his immutable confidence, his self-assurance.

'I don't know if I liked him all that much, actually,' I admitted. 'I think I just wanted to impress him, because he seemed like the kind of person who was difficult to impress.'

'I wonder why it is important for you to impress people,' she said obtusely.

The other women nodded appreciatively.

'This is a pivotal age, twenty-six, my goodness!' Josephine continued, shaking a fist, her voice suddenly preaching. 'You should be excited. This is your opportunity to learn what you want out of life. This is *your* time, to seek out your passions and desires. Love can follow afterward.'

A weak applause came from Dina and Martha. Shauna joined in self-consciously. I was embarrassed by this forced enthusiasm. I smiled thinly. In my head, I tried to imagine a life where I prioritised my passion, something unknown to me, but the void was filled with a dense, black matter.

'We can help you understand yourself, to understand why you allowed yourself to be treated so poorly by a partner,' Josephine said. 'Also, it goes without saying, a period of time free of romantic relationships is important, just so you can clear your head. Try six months, see how it feels.'

At the end of this first meeting, I was hesitant to return. It wasn't just the dusty carpet and misspelled motivational quotes tacked to the wall. I found myself unwilling to accept affection from these women, people whom I was frightened to identify with. Did I really believe they ought to accept themselves? Would I want to love myself, in their circumstances?

I said as much to Martha on the phone afterwards and was puzzled by her drawn out silence.

'Are you still there?'

'Yes. I'm just surprised by your outlook,' she said.

'How so?'

'Well, what is it about them that makes you think they don't deserve to be loved?'

'No,' I said, 'I just mean I'd find it hard to feel good about myself, if I was them.'

'Oh, because you feel so good about yourself now, right?'

I began to dispute this, but she interrupted me. She said she was busy and had to rush off.

It was this that made me decide I'd return, to try and finish this conversation she had started between us.

*

For the next six weeks, I joined Martha at several spin classes a week, as well as early morning body-conditioning sessions. I bought a Himalayan salt lamp, a diffuser and a tiny bottle of expensive facial serum. I also found a new job as a sales assistant in a jewellery shop, following a spell of sporadic office temping. My co-workers were both female aged forty-five and seventeen, and our giddy and conspiratorial dynamic was that of an aunt and her two nieces. I stopped reading in bed and instead started watching movies like *Steel Magnolias* and *Terms of Endearment*. In the group, I let myself feel enveloped by female friendship, something that I had only ever seen as a consolation prize in the wake of a failed romance.

Initially, I felt excited by what I saw as nascent spiritual growth. But I soon began to see that real growth was elusive. The changes I had made lost their meaning when I realised that they were only significant if other people noticed them, which they rarely did. It had nothing to do with improving my relationship with myself. The salt lamp couldn't distract from the general disorder of my room, the skincare products failed to transform my often-greasy pallor. In just a matter of weeks, my job became boring and easy, and I spent most of my time thinking about what I'd eat for lunch. Yes, I had stronger legs from the gym classes, but my ass was still covered in cellulite, so what was the point? Bored of the stories of uncomplicated platonic and familial love between stoic Southern ladies, I returned to my Angela Carter and Penelope Mortimer books. But I couldn't concentrate, my sensibilities had been altered; the dense and bleak subject matter now made me feel stupid and afraid.

'Create a vision board,' Josephine suggested when I brought up my dissatisfaction. 'One with images that might symbolise the kind of life you dream about.'

For as long as I could remember, all I had ever daydreamed about was romance. In the daydream, things like jobs and friends were incidental, nothing more than an aid to the story: I met him because I went here for this job, he admired me because I did this for that friend. My attachment to my mother wasn't turbulent or obsessive. In moments of doubt or illness, it wasn't her hands or face I imagined, but those of whatever man I had fixed my hopes to at the time.

In an attempt to recapture my earlier commitment and

determination, I bought the materials required to create a vision board. The images my mind conjured were like a still-life composition: a blue tiled counter with a bowl of oranges and a bottle of olive oil sitting on top of it. Maybe I'd swim every day and have several pets, and I didn't know what my job would be. Truthfully, I'd have someone who loved me too, but I felt like including this on the board defeated the purpose of the exercise.

Before I could attach the cut-out images, my phone lit up with a notification. It was a message from Richie. I sat, afraid to open it, suddenly embarrassed by the vision board, as if he were in the room watching me tack together pictures of cats and lemons. We hadn't spoken in over three months.

'Are you working in Taylor's Jewellers?' he wrote. My heart started to race.

Then: 'I thought I spotted you when I walked by the shop window but it may have been someone else'. I thought about being seen by him, unaware of his presence, and my face grew hot.

Another message came through: 'Anyway, if it was you, congratulations. I know you hated temping'.

I only hated temping because I felt it was unimpressive and Richie often expressed surprise that I could afford to pay rent with such a low income. In truth, my parents still deposited half my rent in my account every month, but I couldn't tell him this.

I replied to say yes, that was me.

'If you like, I'll come and say hi next time', he replied.

I stood up to pace the floor while replying, abandoning

the unassembled board and the scraps of paper. It wouldn't be discarded or returned to with any real focus. Eventually, it would all be swept aside, beneath the bed.

*

'You are doing the same thing all over again, Alison,' Josephine said.

I tilted my head in sarcastic interest.

Her eyes flashed. 'I can see you are angry with me for pointing this out. But soon enough, you'll have to learn that you can't be a victim forever. If you end up broken-hearted, it won't be Richie's fault. The responsibility lies with you.'

At this, I rolled my eyes. It had been six weeks since Richie and I had started seeing each other again. With Martha I became evasive, telling strange lies, hinting that I might not need to attend the group anymore. Only when she spotted me meeting him at the café around the corner from the gym did she realise.

'Josephine, surely it's healthy for me to navigate a relationship, at some stage? To enjoy something?'

'How very clever of you. You want to have fun, is that it?' She craned her neck forward. 'You made a commitment. If it was meant to be between you and Richie, you could have waited. But you didn't because you are not in control when it comes to him.'

She pointed at Martha then, who averted her eyes. 'And I wouldn't know about any of this if Martha hadn't had the courage to tell us on your behalf. It is a waste of time, lying to us and to yourself.'

I glanced coldly at Martha, which Josephine caught. 'And don't blame Martha either, she did this out of care for you,' she said. 'I cannot force you to change your mind, and I don't see ultimatums as productive. At the end of the day, this will run its course. You may find that this relationship is incompatible with your own journey. How long this will take, I can't say.'

While her dismissal of my relationship frustrated me, I couldn't deny my own doubts. The name-calling during sex resumed. I had previously told myself it didn't matter, that parameters for normality in sex couldn't be prescribed. But now I found myself flinching or receding, unable to remain an active participant. Whether this was because the influence of the group was working, I couldn't tell exactly.

It wasn't unusual for Richie to ignore my messages and evade me for days. This had been a pattern when we first got together, months earlier, and it continued after we rekindled the relationship. Sometimes, a full two weeks might slip by before I'd see him. These episodes were usually preceded by periods of acute closeness. We'd both call in sick for the day, drive to Wicklow, or spend entire weekends in his bedroom. He'd soon be in low spirits though, paranoid, convinced that I'd tricked him into missing work, that I was deliberately trying to distract him.

During the first months of our reunion, I learned that the length of his absence was influenced by how much I fought it. Despite knowing this, I always lingered too long, unable to leave while he still wanted me. I'd wait until he grew restless, until he met my hands and mouth with resistance.

Then that old, inert gloom would drape over me once again. I should have left earlier, I'd think, on my knees, inefficiently gathering a stray sock from under his bed. Occasionally, all he needed was the reassurance that I would go when he wanted me to. Sometimes, this was enough to ease his agitation: the sight of my things tidied into a rucksack. It was just so hard to leave. Even when we'd been together for days on end, it still didn't feel like enough.

*

Three months passed like this, with his coming and going. Gradually, I got used to the cycle of intensity and withdrawal. The anticipation of his absence was always worse than the reality. Even in the midst of the gloom, life went on, I was busy. I took up aqua aerobics with Martha and Shauna. At the jewellery shop, I'd been promoted to assistant manager and my hours had almost doubled. Richie was unimpressed; retail wasn't a career. But it was hard to worry about mediocrity when I could finally afford to pay my own rent.

Very slowly, Richie's tendency to take himself so seriously began to seem foolish and naive. I couldn't bring myself to end it, but the idea emerged time and again from the back of my mind, like a medical appointment I kept forgetting. A boundary line appeared between this relationship and the rest of my life. The line began to thicken and stretch, and I knew that I couldn't straddle it forever, that at some point I'd have to stop delaying.

By then, Richie was living in his parents' house. He had been made redundant at work. He was almost constantly in a bad mood, and I quickly learned not to ask him about it because it only made him blame his unhappiness on me. I think his pride was wounded. He'd assumed he was a valuable asset and it bruised him to see who they had held onto instead of him. For almost six weeks, he refused to let me visit his parents' home.

'There's no point in introducing you,' he said. 'Not since I'll be gone from there soon.'

But the redundancy package was generous, and he wondered if perhaps he should he wait until he secured another job before renting somewhere else. Except, no job paid well enough, or reflected his experience in the way he demanded. Eventually it was agreed that I would be allowed to visit, providing I wouldn't get too close to his mother outside of the usual pleasantries.

I was surprised by how run-down his family home was. He had talked plenty about his parents' working-class origins, how proud he was of where they came from. But I had assumed his father had grafted successfully up a financial and professional ladder despite his lack of education, like the men in Richie's collection of autobiographies about self-made millionaires. It didn't occur to me that his obsession with money might be borne out of insecurity rather than familiarity. His parents' house looked much more like my own family home, a three-bed terrace, with just a narrow strip of grass as the front garden, and this instantly helped me relax.

Richie had spoken with intense emotion about his father's intelligence, his innovative approach to life. His talent was wasted, he explained sadly, he was saddled with a wife and a child, and this had stopped him from reaching his true potential. He shone in his own circles — yes, it was obvious. Everyone knew that Dick Griffin was sharper than most. But his life was weighted by monotonous obligation, and the opportunity to flourish had been stolen from him.

This was something Richie lamented frequently. His biggest fear was wasting his life in a similar fashion. I had been prepared to meet an energetic, intimidating man, someone who required me to match his intellectual agility. I was surprised, then, to be faced with a slight person with a limp handshake, whose eyes couldn't seem to meet mine. After a brief introduction, Dick retreated to the dim sitting room, where a television showed a football match. He lowered himself into his chair, cleared his throat and increased the volume.

Richie's mother Evelyn ran the home with a swift competence. My first impression was that whatever humour or charm he possessed, he had inherited it from her, unknowingly. She asked insightful questions about my work in the jewellery shop, my new duties and my relationship with the staff, all while she washed and polished the dishes from their dinner. She had a skill for hiding her dominance, and I imagined that Richie hadn't recognised it because he was so used to it.

She showed a polite interest and respect for my work, even though I played it down. 'Maybe it's not ideal, but aren't you working?' she said, brightly. 'Aren't you earning your own wage and standing on your own two feet?'

She didn't object when we retreated to Richie's room, didn't insist it was too abrupt an ending. She simply smiled distantly and moved on to the next thing that needed her attention.

Richie's room smelt faintly of dust and socks. Beside the bed was a large suitcase, on top of which several shirts and jumpers had been slung untidily. On the damp windowsill sat a spider, poised and rigid.

'I'm sure you're delighted with yourself,' he said, landing heavily on his bed, which was made neatly.

'How so?' I asked, suddenly afraid.

'Well, you got to have a good nose around, didn't you? I suppose it's not as big as your parents' house, is it? And you and my mam had a good laugh too, at my expense.'

'What? When?' I asked, still standing at the end of the bed.

'Ah, come on, that little comment about standing on your own two feet. That was a dig at me. And you bragging about your job. It just makes me look bad, obviously.' He shook his head. 'I may as well not have even been there.'

'Richie, I think you might be reading into a subtext that doesn't exist. She was being polite. And I was embarrassed talking about my job so much. Jesus, I know it's nothing to brag about.'

'Sure, I know that,' he nodded. 'You probably had every opportunity to do well in life, too, unlike me. It might not look like it now, but I'm not going to let life pass me by. I'm not about to let this setback slow me down.'

I moved closer to the bed and sat beside him. 'I know that, Richie, you don't have to tell me that.'

'Yeah, I do, Alison, because sometimes you need to be reminded that you're not as smart as you think you are.'

'Listen, I never said I was *great* or anything,' I started, but trailed off upon seeing the flat, distant look in his eyes. This was his foreplay; except he had initiated it without asking.

He continued, speaking softly. 'Sometimes, it's as if you forget that I could drop you tomorrow, and it wouldn't mean anything to me.'

This would have hurt more if he hadn't also started rubbing at his crotch through his jeans. He propped himself up and leaned over me. He pulled at my hips, trying to get me to lie down, but I pressed a hand to his chest and tried to sit back up.

'No Richie, not here, I can hear your mam in her room.'

'Good,' he said, yanking my top down over my bra.

'No, it's not good, I don't want it,' I snapped.

'I don't really care what you want,' he said quietly, but he sat back on his heels.

He cleared his throat. 'I'm sorry. You can stay if you like, but I'm not really much company tonight.'

'Well, if you prefer, we can go back to mine,' I said.

'No,' he said, suddenly adamant. 'I've an interview tomorrow and now I'm feeling unfocused.'

'I didn't know you had an interview,' I said.

He shrugged. 'I knew you'd be excited for me. And that would be off-putting.'

Rather than taking this to heart, I felt sorry for him, in a way I never had before.

I had anticipated another protracted period of silence to follow, so I was surprised to wake up the next morning to several messages from him, apologising for his behaviour. I was late for work and decided I could respond later in the day. At lunch, another message came through, asking was I angry with him. The morning had been busy, with many unreasonable customers. My lunch break was brief and rushed. In the afternoon, Martha surprised me by dropping into work, to see if I would like to walk to the seafront that evening. It would be a lie to say I had forgotten about Richie's messages. I switched off my phone, deciding not to think about them until I got home.

That night, I turned my phone on only for a stream of messages to arrive, each varying in length and tone. In some, he realised he hadn't treated me well, that he'd do better in the future. In others, he called me a narcissist and claimed I had unfairly rejected him because he had lost his job. In his final message, he said he was on his way to my apartment, that he needed us to resolve this problem immediately. I considered waking my housemate, or calling Martha. In the end, I pushed a chair against my bedroom door handle. I lay awake for most of the night, furious and afraid, jumping at every noise, startled awake by dreams of being shaken and throttled in my sleep.

When I relayed this to the group the next day, Josephine's eyes were wide and compassionate.

'You still seem undecided. Why is that?' she asked.

'Sometimes, I believe that if I tolerate bad treatment,' I said, pressing my hand to my abdomen, 'it will compensate for what a bad person I am, on the inside.'

Josephine shook her head several times. 'Alison, you have a sheen that you present to the world,' she began, slowly, passing a hand across her face. 'Sometimes, you only allow us to see the charm and the sweetness. But you struggle to ask for help because you are afraid of what people might see underneath the sheen.' She gave me a thin, kind smile. 'There is nothing wrong with you. You just do not want to be known. And this leaves you very alone in your life.'

'Richie is dangerous for you, right now,' she continued, calmly.

I began to speak but she lifted a hand, signalling for me to wait, to listen. 'I'm not saying he is a terrible person. I don't know him, so I cannot say that,' she shrugged. 'But you cannot take care of yourself around him. And each of us is precious, so we must take care of ourselves. And one another.'

'I'll help you take care, Alison,' Shauna said, turning towards me. I knew this was hard for her to say; displays of public affection embarrassed her. Martha, Dina and Johanna murmured their agreement, and it was quiet for a moment.

In the end, I allowed Martha to text him from my phone in the car after group. I asked her to turn off my phone then. Rather than being upset, I couldn't help laughing at this conspiratorial situation we found ourselves in. I kept waiting for him to call, even though I'd blocked the number. I expected him to arrive at my job or apartment, but he never did that either.

*

It would be another seven years before I'd encounter Richie again. At that point, I had been working as a counsellor for nearly three years, having enrolled in college the year after our split. It was a Friday evening in July, 2018, and I was driving to Martha's house in the rain, listening to the radio.

I'd had two particularly heavy sessions that day, one with a new client, a woman whose husband had left her following the deterioration of her health. She had been diagnosed with multiple sclerosis a few years earlier, and when she had been well, he had promised to stand by her. This was no longer the case, now her condition had worsened.

The other client was a woman I'd been seeing for almost a year. She was a writer who complained that she kept coming up with the same story, again and again, without meaning to. Except, every time she reproduced it, it got worse. Her first published story had been a success, she said, and she found herself trying to replicate it. She was trapped, she explained, because she couldn't quite recapture her earlier skill, but she also couldn't move on to the next thing. She was panicking, worrying she'd never progress from this period of stasis.

When I first started working with this woman, I had privately found her creative anguish boring and self-indulgent. I had other clients who had lost parents and children, who were dealing with illness and marital breakdown. Her introspection irritated me, and she picked up on it, which became a source of insecurity for her, a fear that I was judging her. I try to avoid reassurance when possible, but I did remind her that I wasn't her family or friend; she was paying me to provide a service and it was safe for her to be herself. As the months progressed, I watched my other clients overcome the brutality of their losses and settle into new phases of their lives. In almost every case, the things that tripped them up were the small humiliations, the loneliness of their day to day.

I knew the fear of inadequacy. As our work together progressed, I began to wonder why I'd been so cool with the writer, reminding her of the professional boundary, when what she'd needed was an extended hand. I felt fresh empathy for her, and saw that in the absence of disease and death, there were always other little heartbreaks and grievances that demanded our attention.

The traffic was terrible, and I was tired. I would have preferred to go right home, but this would be the first time I'd seen Martha since her wedding a month ago. She was pregnant, but it was very early, and she'd had two miscarriages previously, so she was cautious. She had left the group three years ago and I followed shortly afterwards. Josephine had started to ask people to sign up for a monthly direct deposit, to help fund the growth of the group. She wanted us to enrol our friends and family too. She aspired to create a community of supportive, self-reliant women.

Martha's scepticism was honest and uncomplicated. 'It was about to become a cult,' she'd said sadly, 'and I couldn't aid that.'

'If it was a cult,' I'd said, 'then it's a real shame, because I think my life would have been a lot worse without it.'

On the radio, an exuberant DJ introduced the next guest to his show, a man who had apparently made huge waves as an online personality and stand-up comedian. 'I'm sure many of you know him from the brilliant sketches that went viral earlier this year. You're very welcome to the show, Richie Griffin.'

At first, the name struck me as only vaguely familiar. It wasn't until he started speaking that I recognised who he was. I was surprised by his earnestness, his charming self-deprecation. This was shortly after the abortion referendum. He joked with the DJ about his father's efforts to understand the cultural significance, the punchline proving more endearing than funny. When I knew Richie, he was indifferent about the right of a woman to choose. He called it a middle-class problem and ridiculed me for becoming emotional in the face of his disinterest.

'I'm not your *foe*,' he'd said, 'calm down.'

I left Martha's later that evening without telling her what I'd heard. In the coming days, I googled his name and discovered that he'd recently enjoyed mild success through the short videos he made about his awkwardness, his inability to talk about his anxieties and frustrations. Honestly, he was less of a comedian and more of a mental health advocate, which I supposed wasn't uncommon among online personalities.

I found three recent podcast episodes that featured interviews with him and listened to all of them in one evening as I washed the dishes and walked my dog and put away clean laundry. In each interview, he repeated the same few phrases, relying on an effective combination of modesty and vulnerability. I sometimes saw my clients do this too, in an effort to win me over, although I wished they wouldn't. It was evasive and counterproductive. Of course, I understood that I also did this, in my twenties, with Josephine.

I discussed the encounter during a session with my supervisor, Ted, the following week. I wanted to contact Richie, through email, to finally offer my experience of our relationship. Ted discouraged this; he thought it might foster some earlier obsessive compulsions of mine.

'You say it's about closure,' he ventured, 'but I'd argue that it's more about retribution.'

I shrugged, ceding that this could be true, because I'd learnt that it was a struggle and a waste to be dishonest. Regardless, two nights later, I couldn't leave it alone any longer. I scrolled through my inbox, searching for Richie's email address. He probably doesn't even check this anymore, I thought, as I started to draft the mail.

'Hi Richie,' I began. 'I hope it's okay for me to contact you out of the blue like this.' I reminded him, briefly, of our history, something that I found both necessary and faintly embarrassing.

'I heard you on the radio,' I continued. 'I had no idea you harboured any ambitions to become a comedian.

'I know that I ended things abruptly and without much of an explanation. I wanted you to know that there were a lot of things that happened between us, both sexually and emotionally, that made me unhappy. I couldn't tell you at the time because I believed I wasn't worth better treatment.'

I went on, saying that I didn't expect an apology, or a reply. I wasn't even trying to convince him he should feel remorse. 'I just thought that if I have to be faced with unexpectedly seeing you on television, or hearing your voice on the radio, I should at least allow myself to be honest about my perspective, even if our relationship ended a long time ago.'

I signed off as 'Your Reluctant Spectator'.

I thought that if I were to receive a reply, it might be

weeks later, that my message might be something he'd avoid addressing, until the dread became too overwhelming. I was surprised then, to see a new email land in my inbox forty minutes later, from Richie. It occurred to me, just before opening it, that my email could be perceived as a threat, that he might think I was swooping in now to destroy his chance at fame with revelations of coercion and mistreatment. Given the level of paranoia he had been prone to when I knew him, it wouldn't have surprised me.

'Hello Alison,' he began. 'While it made me sad to read how much I hurt you, I am still happy that you got in touch. I haven't thought about you in a long time, but I do have happy, if conflicted, memories of our time together.'

The words struck me as stiff and impersonal, as if I were an ailing aunt rather than a person he used to spit on during sex. For a ridiculous moment, I wondered if he had asked Evelyn, his mother, to write it for him.

'Of course, there is no need to remind me how badly it ended,' he continued. 'I also know that my behaviour was unacceptable, both throughout our relationship and as it drew to an end.

'I'm sorry that you had to be confronted with my presence once again, unexpectedly. I understand why this would be painful and frustrating.'

At this point, I paused reading, to consider my emotions. I had largely dealt with my previously low self-esteem, through therapy, yes, but mostly through growing up. All that remained was curiosity, so I continued to read.

'I was very insecure about my sexuality and felt unable to talk about it. I started to resent you because I saw you as being complicit in how I treated you, because you allowed me to treat you badly. I know this isn't right and it may be hurtful to hear, but I'm just trying to explain my thoughts at the time.

'I think, if I'm honest, I wasn't entirely attracted to you. You made me feel as though what I was doing was okay and so I think I just felt comfortable around you. This led to me taking advantage of you and for that, I am so sorry.'

Once I reached the end, I read it again immediately. I felt mildly stunned, the way you might if you saw a celebrity in the queue ahead of you in the supermarket. I suppose he was perhaps on the cusp of celebrity status. Other than that, I felt very little, and slept through the night.

The next morning, I busied myself with cleaning the bathroom, knowing that I needed to challenge the compulsion to keep reading our emails, over and over. While pulling some tangled wet hair out of the shower drain, I remembered an idea Josephine shared with us, years earlier, about how we see ourselves. Self-image was just one half of a split screen, she'd said, with her usual passion and emphasis. On one side of the screen, you saw yourself in focus, poised and deliberate, your intentions and purpose clear. I recalled how she'd drawn her narrow shoulders back, to embody this image. On the *other* side, she'd said, was how the rest of the world saw you. The footage was fleeting, panned across your blurred face – it was *artless*. What could you do? She'd shrugged, closed her eyes. Nothing. You had no say in how the world saw you.

I read Richie's email once more. I began to type a reply: 'I am happy that you are being truthful.' I deleted this sentence immediately, recognising this approach as excessive and a little pathetic. I spent the morning considering what I'd say instead, analysing his potential reaction and how he might respond, how the conversation might evolve and continue. I was trying to course correct, to pick up the thread of a conversation that was never going to happen between us. What I'd wanted, I realised, was for him to say he thought about me a lot, that he considered my life a success. He hadn't even asked about my life. Instead, he'd managed to deliver an apology and an insult in one line, something that moments earlier I'd been about to thank him for.

It was almost noon on Saturday before I abandoned my drafted reply altogether. It had been over a week since I'd let this consume me. I got on with the cleaning but found myself checking my inbox frequently. The empty draft still sat there, days later. I forced myself to delete the thread of our conversation because, even though I knew it almost by heart, I kept rereading it, as if this time we might say something different.

Lines to Keep

All morning, Greg kept talking to his daughter, Jamie, but she wouldn't stand still. She provided brief answers to his questions but otherwise remained silent. He could neither recall the precise moment her mood had soured nor identify the reason why.

'Have you many hours at work this week?' Greg's question was measured and tentative, which irritated her.

'Twelve, I think,' she lied, doubling the true number.

After rinsing his hands at the sink, he turned off the tap and shook away the excess water. He wiped his palms across his shirt and trousers. 'Aren't you there longer than that other girl?'

'*What* other girl?' She knew who he meant, but wanted to expose his uncertainty.

'Ah, you know, the chatty girl, the one from Latvia,' he said.

'Estonia,' she corrected him, although she wasn't sure either.

Jamie laid out four rashers on the pan. Her father stood

watching the strips of meat buckle and shrink on the heat as Jamie turned from the cooker to the cutlery drawer and then to the press to find a plate. Greg leaned against the fridge and looked to the ceiling, drawing a hand across his mouth. She turned the rashers with a fork. Spotting a piece of food that had been flattened into the linoleum, he bent at the waist to scrape it away with his thumbnail. As he straightened up, his knees cracked painfully.

'Good *God*,' he laughed ruefully. Jamie did not acknow-ledge this. The kitchen was quiet for a long moment.

'You would think that man might have more loyalty to his staff. The ones there the longest, I mean,' he said even-tually, reinvigorated with fresh disapproval.

'I can't work more than twelve hours a week anyway. I'm in the middle of exams,' Jamie told him.

'Ah, Jamie, you're not studying medicine, love.' He started to laugh but stopped abruptly. This was a fragile and precarious edge he was negotiating.

'Oh sorry, Greg, I forgot that you're the authority on third-level education, given your vast experience of it.'

She could see that the sudden violence of her words had upset him, and she regretted drawing attention to his lack of education. She didn't usually express herself so explic-itly. She plucked the rashers off the heat and moved the pan from the cooker to the sink. The hot oil spat and hissed as she ran water onto it.

In their narrow kitchen, she sidled past him with a plate of food. She held her breath, waiting for him to ask where she was going, but he didn't say anything. As she climbed the stairs, she could still see him, pinching the bridge of his nose, trying to remember what he had planned to do next.

Back in the kitchen, Greg lay the rashers and some bread on a napkin rather than a plate. He ate the food in five quick bites, at the counter. Their home was clean and simple and smelled like cigarette smoke. For many years, he had been a heavy smoker. He wanted a cigarette then, but in recent years had limited himself to three a day, in a reluctant effort to improve his health. He saved smoking for the evening, his favourite time: he'd have one immediately after dinner, another with a cup of coffee and the last one shortly before bed. The one with coffee was the best. He smoked in the sitting room, taking frequent pulls so that the length of the cigarette didn't dwindle and waste, brushing the ash from his lap. He really loved cigarettes. If he made it to seventy-five, he had decided, he'd smoke as much as he wanted, from morning to night.

Greg used the napkin to sweep the crumbs from the counter into his palm and emptied them into the bin. He thought maybe there was some horse-racing on the television but first he needed the toilet. He climbed the stairs quietly; he was heavy-footed, and he knew Jamie needed to focus. His bladder was aching but it took some time for the release to come, which he'd noticed happening more often lately. Eventually it came, and he shuddered during the last few drops. Only seven more years until he could smoke as much as he wanted.

He felt an ache in his ankle as he walked, haltingly, down the stairs. He'd been to a salsa class recently, his first one ever, and was still stiff from the confused jerking movements. There had also been community gardening and pottery classes and lectures about the town's history delivered by academics in the parish hall. His new friend, Pauline, had no shortage of energy. He'd met her at a local walking club, something he'd been driven to by the relentless boredom of his forced retirement. He had been a painter for forty-two years and last year had fallen from a ladder, shattering several ribs. He still attended weekly physiotherapy sessions and had learned that using the steam room in his local pool gave him great relief from his laboured breathing.

The night that Pauline referred to as their first date was actually an evening spent with the walking gang at a pizzeria. Greg felt self-conscious about eating with his hands in a restaurant around new people. It seemed to be something everyone else did with ease but to him it felt coarse and ungainly. And then there was Pauline's forthrightness, her inability to identify or respect another person's reluctance to answer so many personal questions in a group setting. At one point, amid all the chatter and clattering of plates, he saw her point a circular pizza cutter at another woman before asking, 'Are you wearing a *wig*?'

She had been the one to pursue him, often showing up to the house unannounced, carrying some sugar-laden cake she'd bought at the petrol station, something neither of them would eat. It caused in him an agitated sort of excitement; he didn't like to be surprised with company, but he was often immediately relieved when she arrived: the anticipation was over. This made him think he hadn't really wanted an evening alone, that he'd likely been using cigarettes as a way to pass the time.

Pauline was a widow and she enjoyed her money, knowing how to spend it well in decent restaurants and seaside hotels. She seemed to be under some illusion that, because Greg was also retired, he too was comfortable with spending money. The truth was he struggled along week to week, and it surprised him how fluently he had managed to shield this fact from her. He was too young to stop working and too old to have a child who needed help getting through college. If he was honest, his limited smoking had more to do with the price than anything else (it broke his heart a little, the cost going up so much, since he enjoyed it so thoroughly). In the early weeks of their friendship, he'd allowed Pauline to think he was well-off, pushing away the idea that he ought to be honest about what he could afford. He paid for dinners and drinks with an artificial ease, as though he had no idea exactly how much money he had in his account.

The idea of being honest, of explaining that his situation wasn't quite as comfortable as he'd made it out to be, filled him with dread. It would be such a complicated conversation, each question leading to another, revealing more and more about how precarious things were for him and Jamie and how reckless his recent spending was in light of this. There was still a lot of debt looming over their house, thanks to his previous delay tactics. He was behind schedule and had overestimated his resources. It was something he worked hard to conceal, even from himself, because to look at the numbers, things that were indifferent to his trepidation, was to be frightened and ashamed.

He was in trouble and he knew it; losing the kindness and admiration of Pauline was the least of his problems. He'd have to be honest with her, to explain that this wasn't the right time to be swanning around restaurants and wine bars as if he weren't a poor man. 'Pauline, I haven't a red cent.' He practised saying it, knowing as he heard her car pull into the driveway as it usually did around this time on a Saturday that he'd have to communicate this. He'd planned to do it today, in fact. But then as he watched her approach him, her lips curving in their usual irrepressible cheer, he felt foolish for worrying so much. In his heart of hearts, he believed she already knew his true circumstances, given she had seen how modest his home was. His fears, which were clear to him in her absence, became murky and inaccessible when he was in her company. Yet again, he decided he didn't need to reveal anything, he could let it go for now, batting away the vague knowledge that the same fears would return to him again once she was gone.

*

That afternoon, Jamie borrowed her father's car to drive to her shift at the newsagent's. She was glad to leave when she did, her departure coinciding with Pauline's arrival, a woman she avoided when possible. It was awkward to watch Pauline smiling in wide-eyed alarm at their spare and simple home with so few furnishings and ornaments. Their appliances were cheap and frequently broken. There wasn't a proper shower, just a bath tub with a rubber hose attached to the faucet. It wasn't homely and there was something unsuitable about the place, as though it were fit for college students, yes, but not a family. It embarrassed Jamie, having another woman witness the makeshift conditions that she and Greg had grown so accustomed to. Jamie felt exposed, as though she had been failed by some feminine instinct that had never kicked in.

Then there was Greg, who thought he could convincingly shape the place up with pound shop pillows and scented candles. There was also the novelty pepper grinder that was at least ten inches tall, an item he'd purchased while in Northern Ireland. Recently, when he and Pauline had eaten pasta in the garden together, Jamie watched from her bedroom window, mortified, as he brandished the pepper grinder, twisting the head of it with great pride over Pauline's bowl.

It was unsettling, to see him lead such an active social life with Pauline, when in years prior to that he'd seemed to have no interest in holidays or eating out. It surprised her to hear him lament their lack of money, lately; there was a faint bitterness in his tone that she thought uncharacteristic. She experienced something adjacent to jealousy and possessiveness, a resentment she traced back to the loyalty she felt towards her mother. Their marriage had not been a loving one, and it was obvious to most people that her mother was an angry and unhappy woman, with little time or patience for children, including Jamie. Her mother was twelve years younger than Greg. The origins of the relationship seemed unclear, but Jamie knew that they'd got married when her mother was pregnant, throwing a small party in a pub after the church.

Her father had been content with the situation, expertly extracting himself from the room when his wife flew into a fit of rage or despair about their home, their life, her future. Rarely had he let it bog him down; he was quick to forgive. Yes, he had been satisfied with their old life but now, he did not appear to miss her mother. It seemed to Jamie that he lacked a certain object permanence: once a thing was taken away, he got over it quickly and accepted the present for what it was.

And now, he seemed happy again, with a woman who was entirely different to her mother, a woman he took out to dinner and the cinema. In hindsight, Jamie felt a strange sort of pity for her mother because he had never offered to do these things with her. It wasn't as if she ever asked, but he could have tried, he could have taken some initiative. And maybe if he'd had the courage to try, she might have felt valued and less overwhelmed by regret.

Jamie had worked in the newsagent's for two years. Greg was right, she needed more hours so she could save money for the postgraduate course she hoped to do next year. Greg was incredulous that she'd need this qualification to become a teacher.

'Tell me again how education in this country is free, just try,' he'd said.

She could have used her wages to rent student accommodation, somewhere closer to the university. At least then she could have also worked in the city. But the idea panicked her; it seemed indulgent and overwhelming. She usually got the bus to college, which picked her up at eight in the morning and then didn't drop her back home until six in the evening. There were some days she might only have one or two lectures, which meant there was a lot of hanging around on campus and in the library, but it was worth it — she didn't like to miss any classes.

Lately, her job had become more difficult because a newly appointed manager, Peter, had reduced her hours yet again. Peter was in his late twenties. The only person older than Peter was Janet, the lady in her fifties who didn't seem to remember Jamie's name and never wanted to swap shifts or take on extra hours because she frequently had to look after her grandson. Jamie had applied to several other jobs in the town, but it was almost summer, so there were a lot of students around and most of them needed work.

All the boys liked Peter because he didn't pretend that his job was more important than it was. He acted like he was reluctant to order anyone around and even the more timid girls thought he was nice. He teased everyone, so for the first little while Jamie had tried not to take it personally. A lot of the people she worked with could give as good as they got but Jamie couldn't pull it off. She tried to tease him back but then she worried he might think she was flirting. Peter seemed to be offended by her reluctance to participate and this only provoked him more. She hated how stiff and brittle she appeared in these interactions; she knew that it made her seem strange and solemn.

Peter would look you up and down at the start of his shift, and if he noticed something different, like maybe your shoes were a bit clumpy or your hair was greasy, he'd be sure to mention it. Jamie worked with this guy, Alan, who was a little nerdy and awkward. He had really bad acne and his face was constantly red and inflamed. Sometimes he'd be bleeding if he had picked at or scratched at his skin too much. His chin and cheeks were covered in shiny, painful-looking yellow and pink pimples. It was the first thing you'd notice if you were talking to him, of course it was, but you'd never say anything.

'Alan, your skin would probably clear up if you just washed your face once in a while,' Peter told him, right in front of the rest of the staff.

They'd been having a laugh before that, and Jamie could see Alan's smile freeze on his face. She knew he was thinking, Oh, no, please, tell me I misheard him. His face flushed bright red, and he didn't say anything, just continued sliding cereal boxes onto the shelves.

'No, really,' Peter continued, moving closer to Alan. 'I'm not trying to insult you. I'm just saying you'd look better without all those spots, you know,' he said, running a hand over his own jaw and cheek.

The worst part of it was that Alan's skin started to clear up after this. It was probably just that his hormones had settled down, but everyone said it was because Peter had taught him to wash his face.

Peter often tugged at Jamie's collar or her ponytail, and criticised her if she stuttered or tripped over her feet when walking down the narrow aisles. This wasn't so bad: she could put up with that because it wasn't really *about* her — it was for the benefit of everyone else's entertainment. She didn't like being used as a device, of course, but what could she do?

What she really couldn't stand was him following her to the bathroom. He'd lean on the doorframe at the threshold afterwards, blocking her exit, tapping his watch, loudly declaring the visits too long and too frequent. The first time, she could actually feel tears fill her eyes she'd been so embarrassed. He'd feigned shock and regret, telling her he was sorry but that he'd only been having a laugh, and this had made her feel foolish and impotent. The next time it happened, she'd tried to laugh too. But this seemed to offend him, and he'd accused her of taking the piss. And so, from then on, she let herself be startled by him because it was the only way he could find it funny, if she jumped as if she wasn't expecting it at all. She learned that, in order to get it out of the way, she needed to give him exactly what he wanted.

Jamie clocked in fifteen minutes early to her six-hour shift. She did this often, to accumulate extra time on the clock. She immediately checked next week's roster, scanning the list for her name. Peter had scheduled her for four hours next week, the fewest she had ever been given. Although she'd only been contracted to work four hours a week before he'd started, she usually worked at least sixteen. Lately, she had been averaging six hours per week, which was not enough. Looking at the roster, she tried to disguise her disappointment.

She was reluctant to approach Peter, and an hour passed before she forced herself to seek him out. When she tapped on the door to the office, which was open, all he said was 'Yep!' without looking up from the computer.

'I just wanted to let you know that I'm free for more hours, if anything comes up,' she said.

'There probably won't be any more than what's there, unless someone calls in sick,' he said absently.

'Well, you might keep me in mind anyway,' she said. 'I'm scheduled for four hours next week and that's the lowest I've ever been given.'

He swung around in his chair and sighed. 'I prioritise the full-time staff. They are available when I need them and they don't pick and choose their schedule so if there's hours free, I'm more likely to give them to them.'

'Well, I'll be off college for the summer soon, so I'll be available full-time too,' she said.

'Sorry, are you the manager now? Do you want to try to schedule the roster for next week, is that it?' He stood up, gesturing toward his chair, as though to offer it to her.

She stepped back and shook her head mutely.

He sat back down and faced the screen. 'I'm busy at the moment,' he told her.

She turned to leave but he called after her. 'And Jamie? Stop clocking in early. If I schedule you from two until six, just work those hours.'

*

When Jamie arrived home that evening, Greg was alone, singing in the kitchen while he washed some dishes in the sink. There were a couple of empty cans of Guinness on the kitchen counter, as well as a half-empty bottle of wine. She could hear horse-racing on the television in the sitting room. As much as he seemed to enjoy having Pauline over, he also seemed relieved to have her leave, as if he had successfully gotten through another encounter and could relax.

'Hey, J!' he called out, leaning away from the sink to get a look at her.

She saw that his shirt was soaked and rumpled and knew that he'd been drying cutlery on it again, something she couldn't scold him for because she hadn't witnessed it. She told him, multiple times, not to do that.

'That was a short one,' he said, walking towards her. He held both shoulders and tried to kiss her forehead. 'It feels like you only left an hour ago. Still, great that you're off for the evening.'

She pulled away, irritated with him for his good mood.

'Are you working tomorrow?' he asked.

'No,' she sighed. 'That's my only shift this week.'

'You're joking me,' he said. 'What use is that to you? It would hardly cover your bus fare.'

'He said he has to prioritise the full-time staff,' she told him.

Greg winced. 'See, Jamie, I told you, you needed to make yourself more available. He's not going to do what suits you, he doesn't care that you're in college.'

'What was I supposed to do? Drop out for a job in a crappy little shop?'

'Jesus, did I say that? I'm just saying you could have maybe missed one day in college because you have so few lectures. It hardly makes sense for you to be there when you could be home working.'

The kitchen went quiet and he continued to wash the dishes, breathing heavily through his nose. It was rare that he expressed exasperation because her tolerance for it was so low. Her irritation was palpable.

'It's not like I haven't tried to get another job. I know you don't think that it's important for me to go to college, that you think it's a waste of time, but I don't want to be working in shitty jobs for the rest of my life like you and mam.'

He pressed his lips together in a thin line. 'Jamie, I don't want that for you either. I'm just saying that if you want to do the extra year, you need to save for it, and that job is a handy number for now. So, he's a bit of a prick, who cares? I think you might need to toughen up a little bit, to be honest. Just go in and earn your wage and then you'll be out of there before you know it.'

He thought he was diffusing the situation, making light of it, but before he could continue, she was gone. He heard her footsteps pounding up the stairs.

'Oh, for Jesus' sake,' he said, quietly. It wore him out, it really did.

Carmel, Jamie's mother, had died following a catastrophic brain aneurysm when Jamie was eighteen. When Carmel was alive, Jamie'd spent her time in pursuit of her mother's approval, a delicate endeavour in which she often failed. As a child, her clumsy, breathless dances and senseless plays elicited nothing more than a tired kind of indifference. Carmel's eyes slid past her uneasily, as if Jamie were a hallucination, the consequence of a fever or food poisoning. She would press her fingers to her temple and grip the banister, climb the stairs and shut herself away in her room with the curtains drawn, complaining of headaches, constant, unrelenting headaches.

In hindsight, Jamie suspected this endless malaise was the result of an unrecognised mental illness. Your mam isn't well, was whispered frequently by Greg, who was tasked with entertaining Jamie in her mother's absence. Potato waffles or instant noodles again for dinner. No bed-time enforced. Her mother had had a low tolerance for children. When her patience was tested, she'd struggled to control her temper. Frequent fits of rage over innocuous things: Jamie taking her hairbrush and not replacing it, Jamie spilling toast crumbs on the table without noticing, Jamie dawdling while getting dressed because she got sidelined by a daydream.

'Do you want me to leave? Do you want me to pack my bags and leave?' her mother would cry, her teeth and fists clenched.

At no point had Jamie recognised her mother's threats to leave as empty. Six-year-olds don't think that way, they take their parents at face value. Each time she'd felt like she would puke from crying over the possibility of never seeing her mother again. This upset would only anger her mother further and the arguments would escalate beyond reason. It was just the two of them, in these moments. Greg would slip away, out to the car or the shed.

But then the relief of reconciliation would come, the rush of love between them when they made up. They'd be worn out. Her mother would cry into Jamie's hair, rocking her back and forth. In this state of release, they found the only tenderness available to them, the kind that came about only through cruelty. Greg would return home, grateful that his two girls had worked it out yet again, and he could relax.

*

The next morning, their house was quiet. Jamie regretted snapping but was angry with Greg for his insensitivity. She leaned against the window and drew spirals in the dust on her windowsill. She had yet to make any real start with studying and her exams were looming.

Why had she said anything at all to him? He didn't know about Peter following her to the bathroom; she'd never told him. A small and very young part of her wanted to tell him and for him to be horrified, to promise he would speak to her manager and explain that his behaviour was unacceptable. She was afraid to tell him, in case he told her it wasn't as big a deal as she made it out to be.

It was also likely that he'd resent the sense of obligation that this problem presented. He might feel under pressure to resolve the situation, and pressure usually made him panic. Rarely did he lose his temper, but it was worse that he should abandon her in moments like these. Never once had he stood up to her mother or even told Jamie that the woman's unhappiness wasn't her fault. He'd slip away, closing the door quietly behind him. This had gone on and on until Jamie was a teenager, when she'd no longer needed her mother's affection quite so desperately. She'd never asked Greg why he hadn't taken her away with him. It was never discussed because he considered such conversations overwrought and dramatic. He had a lot of respect for her mother.

She felt uneasy and listless all at once. Instead of opening her books or laptop, Jamie remained leaning against her windowsill looking out to the back garden. The condensation on the glass muffled and distorted her view. She wiped it away with the palm of her hand to reveal Greg in focus, moving along the washing line, pegging clothes in a crowded and careless manner. She watched him finish the task, the line bouncing and bobbing with each addition. He took the basket back inside only to return moments later as a sudden but steady rain shower started.

Greg began to hurriedly remove the clothes and throw them into the basket. He squinted and blinked against the rain. As she watched him, she considered going out to help: he was slow, and the rain was falling heavier. Jamie found she could not make herself do it. A sharp and dense weight settled inside her. He was rushing, which caused him to tremble so much that she could see it from her bedroom window. An acute current of anger arrested her. Only when he looked up to her bedroom window on his way back into the kitchen did she feel it relent. She heard him slam the back door, smack his boots against the mat and call her name from the hall once and then a second time when she did not answer. He called out a third time, louder, his tone conciliatory. She knew that if she went downstairs, there would be no mention of what had happened the night before. She wanted to go to him and match his good nature and yet she could not, she found that she would have no idea where to begin.

Work and Charity

It's a Halloween party and the efforts are sincere and inventive. I'm unhappy with myself for dressing as a ghost: a damp old sheet thrown over my head, two holes cut out for eyes and one for my mouth. I strapped a neon pink bra over the sheet, attached false eyelashes to the eyeholes and applied red lipstick to the mouth hole. It was supposed to be an amalgamation of the spooky ghost and the sexy ghoul, but all the worst parts. There's a competition and I am awarded two cigarettes and five euro for having the laziest costume. The judge is dressed as a martini glass. Inside the cone of plastic wrapped around her waist, a Styrofoam olive rolls back and forth. The edges of the sheet contract and my vision is limited. Friends of friends ignore me, in case they find themselves stuck talking to a stranger.

I spend most of the night with two girls whom I know to be close but competitive friends. They are both emerging as successful artists in Dublin, working in the same discipline. One edges ahead briefly only for the other to overtake her. Their intensity, which presses up against me and crowds me, makes me feel nauseous. The two girls live together, and I cannot imagine that it is a normal arrangement. I assume there is a degree of violence or disgust that must take place privately between them. At the party, I am like a talk-show host, inviting each one to explain their latest achievement, giving each an equal amount of enthusiasm and interest. One of the girls has dressed very convincingly as an elderly woman, the other as a flowerpot.

The flowerpot can't reach her drink as her arms are constricted by the stiff brown drum around her torso. I pass it to her but even lifting it to her mouth seems to be a challenge; the felt petals around her face get in the way. Her father died earlier this year, before the summer. It hasn't interfered with her ambition. Recently, an exhibition dedicated to his memory had been displayed in the National Gallery. One of the pieces was a small furry corpse draped over the shoulders of a mannequin; the flowerpot had fashioned the corpse out of fake fur and plasticine. A note attached to the piece explained that this is how it feels when someone dies: rather than remaining as a spiritual presence, the deceased leaves nothing other than a soft weight around the neck and back of the bereaved. I thought this was a cheap stunt to pull, but only because I didn't believe her.

The flowerpot tells me that her exhibition of grief wouldn't have been a success if she hadn't been so genuinely miserable at that time. I ask her would she prefer to be happy or successful. I'm aware I might come across as especially engaged but I'm just a little drunk.

'Successful,' she says immediately. She refills her drink, takes a brief sip and winces. 'Without a doubt, successful.'

I momentarily feel nauseous. I'd like a cold pint of water. I want to go get some Chinese food, bring it home with me and eat it in bed. The old woman asks me about my job, for the sake of balance. I work at a newspaper, but there isn't much to say and most of it would be a lie anyway. The only thing I could truthfully tell her is that I'm reliable enough to go to work almost every day that I'm supposed to, with clean teeth and tidy hair.

In the bathroom, I gather the sheet around my waist to pull down my jeans. There's a lot of people in the house now and so much noise, all of it unintelligible yelling.

I don't go to the pub after the party. I return home to the room I rent in Harold's Cross. I pull the sheet over my head and pile it in a corner, on top of some dirty socks and t-shirts. I never bothered buying shelves, so there are make-up palettes and brushes balanced on stacks of books beside the mirror. The light bulb has blown and I keep forgetting to buy a new one. All I have is the bedside lamp. Every night I go to switch on the light and then stand in the dark like an idiot. Earlier that day I was probably looking at useless accessories like pillows or mason jars when I should have just remembered to buy a light bulb. I keep doing this stupid thing where I buy cheap ornaments from charity shops, hoping to achieve a run-down-but-original kind of aesthetic. It's obvious that I'm trying to replicate something I've seen on television, about spirited poor people who get it together in the end. Anyway, it never looks right because the room is too shabby and I have bad taste. It would be more effective to keep it clean and save the money for practical, significant purchases.

I have frequent attacks of doubt during the night, or early in the morning, between waking and sleeping. Six months ago, I stopped speaking to my friends from home. When they phoned me after work, I didn't take their calls because I wanted to watch television instead, so that was that. This decision has left me on the periphery of another group, people I didn't know until I moved to Dublin. I cannot keep up with them. I feel like somebody's aunt, kind and inquisitive, but not someone you want to spend the entire night with. They do a lot of cocaine but always bypass me because they know I don't like it. If a friend of a friend offers it to me, they are discreetly scolded, as if they've made a clumsy joke about something personal or sensitive. They all do so much of it and I don't know how they function, excel even. Many of them are succeeding as artists and musicians and by occupying themselves with other things that I didn't even realise could be forged into a living. One girl makes her money by selling homemade framed needlework patterns and printed tote bags. She told me once that she does most of the work while watching television, specifically reality shows about European women who marry older Americans for a visa.

I don't have any of this vigour. I'm usually tired and could always get more sleep if any was available. And, really, I don't think I would like any intimate friendships. They often involve too many expectations and resentments. I am more interested in brief connections, the kind made in airports or waiting rooms.

Monday to Friday, I take the bus at half-seven, which at that hour of the morning smells like soap and bad breath. It travels for a long time, through the city and out to the edges, where things are flat and commercial. Once I'm at my desk, I make gentle and useless enquiries. I'm a bad journalist because I'm afraid of upsetting people. Where others see a trail of questions to be followed, I see a series of boundaries, the breach of each one more offensive than the last. I feel sympathy for slumlords and employers who offer staff very little money and even less security. I feel I ought to give them fair warning. I preface every accusation with an apology and pose it as a question, hoping they'll feign shock in return, as if they knew nothing about it.

Most of the stories I write are about minor injustices that no one will care about. The last one was a price comparison of dentist consultations throughout Dublin. Before that, it was the same but with bin-collection companies. When I first started, the picture editor asked me to visit a department store in town and pretend to be a sixth-year student. I was instructed to try on different school uniforms in the dressing room and note the price of each one. I was also told to take photos of myself in each uniform. This was four years ago, when I had been twenty-four. When I submitted the photos and prices, he looked briefly puzzled and then dismissed me, saying flatly that it had only been a joke.

I try to convince myself that my own story pitches are simply too nuanced but suspect that the fact that they keep getting rejected has more to do with their obscurity and my weak delivery.

'Who cares?' asks Claire, the pregnant editor, every time I suggest something.

My pitches get meeker and more anxious every time, as I anticipate the rejection. I would prefer to say nothing, but we are required to submit three story ideas at the weekly meeting.

'Charity mugging.' Claire points a half-eaten bagel in my direction at the latest meeting. '*Chugging*, that's what I want you to do next. It's when companies pay people to stand in the street and hassle passers-by, raising money for endangered animals and the likes.'

I take fake notes. I just need to do something with my hand to look like I am interested in my job.

'So, what you'll do is enrol with them, get on their pay-roll. Find out how much it pays and where the money *really* goes,' Claire says.

'Okay, sure. But it's just, I suppose, doesn't a portion of the money go to the employees? And then some to the general running of the organisation, and then the rest goes to the monkeys and tigers and that kind of thing.'

'But I want you to find out how *much* goes to the employees. Here's an application form.' She hands it to me sharply.

I wait until the end of the week to fill out the application. I hope that this job will unexpectedly require a long list of qualifications and experience that I don't have. Or that they'll be completely overwhelmed with applications and I'll never hear from them. It will be so much worse than having to bother people over the phone. I'll have to physically block their path and bother them face to face and ask them for their time and their *money*.

I get a phone call the following Monday from a friendly Australian named Sam.

'We were impressed by your application. We'd love to bring you in and have a chat about our current opportunities.'

I wince at this attempt to flatter me: my fake application shows an employment gap of two years. It makes me think less of him already.

'Come on in tomorrow, noon okay for you? And we'll see about getting you started.'

*

The company is actually a hired firm, working on behalf of lots of charities. It isn't so much that I suspect Sam has polished his answers: he just seems to be telling the truth. The firm receives a fee from the charity. This fee is used to pay me and other employees the minimum wage to stand on the street and encourage people to sign up for a direct debit payment for a minimum of twelve months. The money collected is then funnelled straight back to the charity. I know that chugging is considered a nuisance, but I can't help but feel like this isn't an unreasonable way to make money. Perhaps if I could properly consider their overall earnings against the amount of money *given* to the animals, I might feel differently. But then I would also need to compare this with other companies doing the same thing. I can't apply any more pressure or ask any further questions without seeming too hostile or strange. Sam appears to be genuinely passionate about the work he does, and I find myself mirroring him in order to make a good impression. I quickly feel as though this is my real job. When he finishes the introduction to my role, I remark on how much there is for me to learn, that I'll do my best. I can tell my humility has pleased him.

'Of course, the first day is overwhelming,' he says, 'but you'll do well here.'

They provide a yellow bib and instruct me to shadow an energetic American man named Ross. He's been here a little over three months and he tells me this as if it's a long and considerable tenure. Outside the GPO on O'Connell Street, I waver near Ross, growing more and more embarrassed each time I try to match his efforts to elicit acknowledgement from people passing by. It's two o'clock in the afternoon in the middle of November. It's busy with office workers and students and shoppers turning off Henry Street. Recognising the yellow bibs, they pivot around us. Ross pursues them anyway.

'Hi there, have you got a moment to talk about the endangered animals of Sumatra?'

'Oh, hello, you look like you care about elephants! Free for a chat?'

'Would you like to help save an orangutan and her babies this Christmas?'

'No? Okay, that's cool! Have a great day!'

I would say that the worst part is wearing the Santa hats. That and standing beside Ross, looking bewildered and feeling incompetent. I have a sheaf of forms on which people can fill in their bank details, but I can't ask people to do that. I try waving at passers-by, but my discomfort is obvious. It's cold and I know my posture isn't good. I don't have the energy to pretend I'm excited to convince these people to part with their money, monthly, for a year. What difference does it make? And what difference does it make if I play a part in revealing that this practice isn't helping elephants or monkeys? No one is stopping anyway; they're ignoring the cheerful pleas and assertive greetings. The employees are mostly students, trying to earn money. I take regular breaks to walk slowly to the Ilac shopping centre. I go to the public bathroom, lock the cubicle door and sit on the toilet seat for as long as I think I can get away with.

Each morning I wake up and am shocked that I have to keep doing this. By Thursday, I am already certain that I won't succeed in forging an interesting or even viable story out of this experience. Not only have I been unable to fully grasp the structure of the firm and the flow of its finances, I have also failed to sign anyone up to give ten euro a month to endangered animals. Surely, I will be sacked from both jobs.

The only thing that brings normality or comfort to this experience is that Ross seems to genuinely like his work. I have a sense that he enjoys leadership and that my obvious disorientation appeals to him. He doesn't mind that I do nothing other than stand next to him. After the rare occasion that a prospective donor stops to engage with him, he turns to talk me through everything he said and why he said it.

'It doesn't always work out but hey, at least I got to talk to them. And maybe next time they might part with a little bit of cash.' He rubs his fingers and thumbs together and winks at me before turning to shout hello at the next person walking by.

I feel guilty for letting him think I am impressed by his optimism. For his sake, I am glad that none of this will be published.

We finish up close to six. It's dark and drizzling. I usually walk alone to the train after returning my untouched pile of direct debit forms to Ross. Tonight, he asks me if I'd like to go for a drink.

'I feel bad,' he says. 'It's your first week and nobody brought you for lunch or anything.'

I feel bad too because I don't deserve this consideration. I agree to go for a drink and try to pretend it's under normal circumstances. We go to an old pub with a rustic interior that I think is intended to be traditional. It's dark and cramped and reminds me of a spaghetti Western. Ross suggests sitting in the snug. I'd assumed we'd sit at the bar and the drink would be quick, accompanied by a cursory chat. We sit opposite each other. I learn that Ross is thirty years old and from Atlanta, Georgia. I tell him that this surprises me as he doesn't have a southern accent.

'I spent a lot of time in Indiana, with my grandparents. Me and my dad, we didn't exactly see eye to eye,' he starts slowly and thoughtfully, comfortable with taking his time. 'And once I left school, I just stopped going home to Georgia.'

I sense that he'd like to have permission to expand. To grant it, I say that it must have been tough, to be between two homes like that.

'Yeah, I mean, I definitely took it to heart because my

little brothers never got moved around. So, I sort of spent a lot of time wondering what was wrong with me, you know?'

I try to make an expression of attentive empathy but I'm feeling self-conscious. I don't want the conversation to be overheard by anyone. His problem feels too obvious, my responses cold and unnatural.

'Anyway,' he concludes, clapping his hands together abruptly, 'I'm here now, so fuck it, right?'

He lifts his glass and I lift mine too, knocking it against his in agreement.

I think I am a bad person. I worry too much about what people think, making constant adjustments between the thoughts I conceive and how I express them.

Ross leans in like he's about to ask something personal.

'Hey, you don't need to be somewhere, do you? It's just, I'm getting hungry. Is it cool with you if I order some food?'

All they have are crisps and toasted cheese sandwiches. I eat the crisps; he gets a sandwich. We keep drinking. Up until this point, I have been too tense and guilty to wonder if he finds me attractive. He eats very quickly and talks with his mouth full, so probably not. But he conducts himself with a general coarseness and I don't know if this lack of self-consciousness indicates anything other than inalienable confidence. He wipes his mouth roughly with a napkin and laughs, leaning back to lengthen and stretch his torso. He has a weak chin and I don't like his lips; they're too big. He reminds me of a celebrity or a politician, but I cannot place who just yet.

I make a conscious decision to like him, to find him attractive. He isn't very funny so it's hard. He quotes a lot of funny people, but this isn't the same thing. He makes an effort to co-opt local vernacular. He shoehorns certain phrases into conversations where they are not necessarily relevant and I cannot easily respond. We're talking about where we'd like to be in five years' time. I feel I am expressing a true summary of my anxiety, that I am being myself. Then he interrupts to tell me that I can't waste time, I have to grab the bull by the horns. He angles his glass toward me.

'You might be the one to put your shoes on in the morning but you never know who's going to be taking them off at night, right?'

He has pulled me out of the moment, and I feel embarrassed once more by our conversation, about what we do for money on the street. I believe he uses phrases like these to integrate himself into his idea of what it is to be Irish, to create a sense of connection. But it adds no value and I know he is simply repeating something he heard from someone else and is glad to put it to use. I realise that the excess in our use of language is actually intended to avoid connection, and the directness that it demands. We say things that mean absolutely nothing. Regardless, I am reminded that it's likely we are both pretending, to some extent.

We talk about our favourite television shows. We share an interest in the same comedians, ones who became famous but performed in the same company together beforehand. He references an old clip of one comedian being interviewed on a late-night talk show. The host is hoping to derive some kind of sincerity from the comedian, but he won't oblige; his answers are deliberately strange and obtuse. The host grows increasingly frustrated and embarrassed by the comedian's reluctance to cooperate. Ross assumes I haven't seen it, but I have. My father showed it to me years ago and I now find it more comforting than funny. I tell Ross I know the clip that he's referencing and he doesn't believe me. I'm annoyed at myself for reciting the clip, almost by heart, and for being pleased at his surprise. We're both drunk at this stage and we keep repeating lines from the clip intermittently, to fill a silence. This is what I miss about romance: the exclusivity of private jokes. It isn't necessary for them to be funny.

We've reached the end of things. The empty glasses are swept away and we have to leave. Out on the street, Ross keeps saying, 'Oh, I had one more thing to tell you,' while walking slowly beside me. I slow down too even though it's late and I need to get to O'Connell Bridge and get a taxi. I don't get a sense of finality from anything he says; he isn't wrapping things up. He suggests sharing a taxi and I point out that we're going in different directions.

'Not if we go to the same place.' He rolls his eyes.

I can't bring him to my house, in case he sees my housemates in the morning and they start talking about the paper. I say sure, we can go to yours. It's closer to where we need to get to for work tomorrow anyway.

He rents a cottage on the North Strand from the family of a dead woman who cannot make up their minds and sell it. It's dark and the kitchen is carpeted. I say I like it, to be polite.

'Are you fucking crazy? It's like East Germany in here, I hate it.'

His bedroom is cold because the window doesn't shut properly. All night, I'm trying to figure out who he looks like. I'm sitting on his bed. There's no duvet, just three different coloured blankets thrown over the mattress. He's sitting across from me in a sunken armchair, pulling off one shoe, then the other and then his socks. He stops and leans forward, his elbows resting on his knees. He's still holding a sock and smiling at me with his face tilted to the side. With private relief and satisfaction, I realise he looks similar to another comedian I like, one who impersonates various politicians and celebrities amid scandal on late-night television. Stupidly, this makes me feel better about being here. I think this is something he might find flattering but before I can tell him, he tucks the sock into his shoe and pulls himself off the chair. He stands over me and takes my face in his hands, turns it upwards and starts to kiss me. It's fine but a little horrible because he keeps moaning in my mouth. I get a pain in my neck and stand up. He slips his hand under my shirt.

'Is it okay to take this off?' he asks with a reverence I find off-putting.

I say yes because it would cause less stress to carry on than to say I want to go home, to arrange a taxi. He insists on leaving the light on. On the bed, he runs his hands over me lightly. He maybe intends this to be gentle and sensual but instead it tickles me in an unpleasant way. Before he slips his hand into my underwear, I notice how long his fingernails are. I imagine them inside of me and shudder involuntarily. Ross mistakes this for anticipatory pleasure, as if the idea of sex with him is all too much for me.

'Oh baby, I know,' he says, into my neck.

I wish I had a friend to tell, someone who could understand that I'm not trying to be cruel but that I find the performance of this moment both funny and lonely. Ross has a better body than I do. He is trying to rearrange me into different positions. I can see myself in his mirror and keep trying to lie on my back. It's like wrestling a large, muscular puppy. At one point, he lifts his hand to my neck and squeezes gently. I immediately pull it away.

'What? I thought girls like that,' he whispers, maybe trying to be sexy but instead sounding defensive.

I am surprised by my body's ability to cooperate. I'm not enjoying myself, but I must have a deeper intuition that tells me it will be easier to see this through to the end. This stoicism is what instructs my vagina to carry on facilitating the exchange and I'm glad it saves me the embarrassment of denial. Once it's over, Ross lies on his side with an arm thrown across me. He keeps asking if I liked it, if I came, would I like him to make me come now. I say it was great but no thank you. I roll away and yawn, closing my eyes. He keeps talking, keeps repeating lines from the clip we talked about earlier. Then he starts saying he might like to try stand-up comedy himself, someday. Lots of people have told him he'd be good at it, apparently. I think he'd like me to encourage him, but I don't answer. I pretend I'm already asleep.

When I wake up, I feel perfectly fine until I put the pieces back together again. Ross has rolled away from me and faces in the opposite direction. I pull myself up on my elbows to check what's on the floor around me. The room is still dark. I step over his clothes to reach my bag and find my phone. It's almost six. Instead of dressing in his bedroom, I gather my jeans and top, my shoes and one sock, and take them out to the hall. I cannot find my bra, underwear or the remaining sock but this doesn't matter. I get dressed quietly in the hall. I sling my bag over my shoulder and panic when I realise I can't find my coat. I'm trying to remember if I left it in his room, in which case I'll just abandon it. I'm not sure why but I don't want to wake him up, probably because I never want to speak to him again. I check the kitchen and see it has fallen from the back of a chair to the ground. I pick it up and hurry to the front door. The door has two different locking mechanisms and cannot be easily opened. The turning of one lock needs to coincide with the sliding of another and it is hard to manoeuvre while trying to pull on the door handle. I falter a few times and hear the bedsprings creak upstairs. I realise I am panicking, as if I were being held captive, and feel ridiculous. I try the two locks once more and the door pulls open. I close it gently and turn to run towards Annesley Bridge, trying to get out of sight quickly.

I get the first Luas to Rialto and walk home. By the time I get there, I understand that my behaviour this morning isn't a fair reflection of Ross. I decide I won't be going to work on the street today. I am too sick to pretend I want the job and even without the hangover, I never would have been able to extract the required information to write anything resembling a news story. I have three days to come to terms with this, as well as my potential loss of employment. It's a rolling, precarious contract and I have already felt Claire's shrewd and critical eye observe my conspicuous attempts to get through the day with as little effort as possible. I could move home and live with my mother again. The idea of being hungover on my mother's couch, eating soup and buttered white bread in a clean, warm room, strikes me as not only acceptable but desirable. Every day I wake up and think, I do not want to work. I consider it a remote and indulgent aspiration, which it is. But I have a little bit of money. I could manage for a few months. And then after this transitional period, I wouldn't have to work at a paper. I do not have to be the person that I am. The realisation makes me feel uncharacteristically optimistic and generous, to myself and others. I wait until a decent hour and call my mother to tell her my plan. I am disappointed by her initial bewilderment, but I do not falter and she eventually understands. She never bought my ambition to be a journalist anyway.

'It never suited you,' she says.

It occurs to me that I have let myself down but what does it matter? I imagine what I will pack and what I will throw away.

*

I am confident in my decision until Monday morning arrives and I fall back into my usual routine of gathering my bag and scarf and keys and setting out for work. With each step along the canal, my will to deviate gets weaker and harder to fathom. I decide to wait until Tuesday or Wednesday to hand in my notice. It will already be a bad day. Once Claire discovers how little I did on my assignment at the charity, she is sure to be furious. With any luck, she might beat me to it and sack me. My apprehension spoils the morning commute. I might be able to avoid the worst of her frustration if I try to spin a human-interest angle, an insight into the lives led by the staff at the charity, but even in my desperation I know this is a weak idea. I spend the first hour fidgeting and pretending to read emails.

The ten o'clock meeting arrives and everyone gathers around Claire's desk, which is covered in coffee mugs and a stack of today's papers as well as the Sunday editions. I can hardly concentrate on the agenda that Claire goes through or anyone else's stories.

'I suppose you've already seen this.' Claire holds up a copy of the *Mail on Sunday*.

The lead photo shows the back of someone wearing a neon pink bib. The headline reads 'Chugging: the first YEAR of your donations used to pay charity muggers'.

'What can you do? Slow time of year, everyone's just trying to fill the paper.'

I nod eagerly.

'Just pick up the pace next time. We definitely wouldn't have used it for a Sunday paper, but we could have had this out by last Friday if you had got a move on with the copy.' She flicks open the *Mail* and scans over the story. 'I would have loved to get in ahead of them.'

'Sorry, Claire.'

Claire gives me a new assignment, yet another price survey, this time of GP consultations, which are apparently rising steadily across the country. I turn to leave, shaking with relief at having been spared humiliation. I am almost back at my desk when she calls out to me, from across the room: 'This probably seems boring to you, but readers do actually care about these things. It's the bread and butter of our jobs and it affects their lives, daily.'

It is unusual that Claire should give my assignment a second thought. It's not until much later that I realise I have not been successful at hiding my lack of interest and motivation. Of course I haven't. The reason Claire has continued to renew my contract is because she pities me and as a result, estimates me to have low ability. I am angry and embarrassed but think she must be right, because for the rest of the day I try to work but lose concentration every few minutes. I wonder who else knows about my laziness. I realise that the lack of consequences has more to do with the kindness of others rather than my ability to lie and obscure facts. How stupid it is, to work hard at doing nothing, when everyone sees right through it.

*

The following week things aren't good, but they are better. My close call has encouraged me to be a bit more organised. I still plan to leave the job but might hold out until the new year. On Thursday evening, I go to town to buy Christmas presents for my mother. I turn off Henry Street to head over O'Connell Bridge. It's so crowded that I don't notice the fluorescent yellow until I'm right in front of one of them.

'Hello, can you spare a moment to talk about endangered wildlife?'

The person who approached me isn't Ross, but I spot him a short distance ahead. He has just been rebuffed by an old woman when I see him look at me. He recognises me immediately and walks over to keep stride with me as I hurry away.

'Hey! It's me, Ross! Hello?' he says when I don't acknowledge him. 'You never showed up, do you know how worried we were?'

'I'm sorry, no, I really can't at the moment. Bye, now.'

'Where did you go? You never came back to us. We didn't know what happened.'

He tries to block my path but I push past him.

'I'm sorry, really, so sorry about that, thank you, I have to go now.'

He keeps walking alongside me. 'If there was something wrong you should have said so. You should have answered your phone, we were really confused.' He sounds hurt and I can't argue with anything he is saying. 'Sam thought it was something I did. I got in trouble because of you.'

We have reached the corner of Bachelors Walk. I have to wait for the green man; there's a lot of traffic. I stare right ahead as Ross stands over me.

'You can't just walk out on jobs. That's no way of doing things, that's not how life works,' he says.

I consider darting into the traffic, taking my chances. Eventually, there is a gap in cars and I can cross onto

O'Connell Bridge. Ross tries to follow me but is deterred by a cyclist who narrowly misses him.

'Unbelievable,' I hear him shout.

My paper shopping bag rips and the gifts I bought drop to the ground. I stoop to gather what I can. People curse me as they step around me on the bridge. I apologise again and again. It takes so long and I keep dropping things. On the ground, the gifts look cheap and generic. I wrap them in what is left of the paper bag and clutch them to my chest. They are awkward to carry. When I get on the Luas, an older man offers me a plastic bag. I say, 'No, thank you,' although I'm not sure why. I sit across from him the whole way home, holding the pile of objects just so, making sure not to let anything slip.

Tiny Wrestler

Diane arrived home to find the house cold and dirty. Her housemates were at their parents' or boyfriends' homes for the weekend. She sat on the couch without taking her coat off. She was bored but too listless to do anything other than scroll through Instagram and Facebook as the room grew dark around her. She clicked into news links that came up on her feed but never finished reading them. She swiped through Tinder but had no messages waiting for her. She checked her emails and picked up her book, reading one page before putting it down again. Diane felt a strange and inert kind of loneliness. It was Sunday and she needed to start a college assignment that was due that week. She had already failed one class and was barely making it through the rest of the course. Dropping out or deferring the year wasn't an option: she would never get the fees back at this stage. The less she did, the more panicked she felt, but she lacked the motivation to make a start on anything.

Diane opened her laptop. Before logging in, she checked

her phone one more time and was glad to see a Tinder notification. It was a message from someone she'd matched with named Rory. Their initial messages to each other were polite and trivial. He wanted to know what she was studying. A short while later he asked the same question again. He might have simply forgotten that she had already told him. Diane assumed it was because he was messaging multiple women at once and had mixed up the conversations. She swiped through Rory's profile pictures and didn't know if she considered him attractive. But that was how she felt about most of the men she encountered online. This particular app was saturated with photos of different people who looked too similar to leave any distinct impression.

Shortly after the benign chat about the specifics of his job, her studies and their living arrangements, she found that he had a good sense of humour and that he seemed to find her funny too. On her way up the stairs, she received another message from him. She sat down halfway up to concentrate on her reply. The back and forth between them was so satisfying and instant that Diane stayed sitting there for almost an hour.

They each wrote so much in their messages that it was difficult to reply to everything they asked about one another. They compared the irritating and disgusting habits of their housemates. She told him she had felt weirdly lonely earlier that day. He told her that he was dreading work the next day, as he had scheduled a meeting with a client who had impossibly high expectations. She admitted she didn't enjoy what she studied and that she was anxious about finding a job in the field when she graduated next year. He told her not to worry, that he and lots of his friends who had graduated and got full-time jobs still felt incompetent and clueless. They briefly segued into talking about the size of the spider she had found in the shower. He offered to come and kill it. By then, she had already crushed the spider with a shampoo bottle. She replied and said no, asking that he come and release it instead.

'Would you lose all interest in me if I told you that I'm really, really into professional wrestling?' he asked. She actually knew a lot about pro-wrestling from her brother: the complex and choreographed grappling, the predetermined winner, the overwrought acting and personas and storylines. It wasn't something she ever had reason to talk about, but she did enjoy it, and she was glad she could say this to Rory.

'I actually really like it too! But I prefer New Japan Wrestling to WWE because the wrestling looks so much more skilful', she replied, before adding 'Not that I'm any expert!'

'I understand why you feel a bit weird about it though: my Dad used to hate that my older brother was so into it and would try to make him watch football or hurling instead', she continued, hoping this was reassuring.

She thought he might be pleased that they shared an obscure interest, but instead he sent an emoji with an eye-rolling expression followed by: 'You are not into pro-wrestling'.

'I am! Honestly, I'm not saying it to make you feel better'.

He replied, 'No, you *think* you're into it. Girls always say they're into gaming or comic books or, in this case, wrestling. They do it to seem unique'.

If he had said this to her face, Diane might have been incredulous or assumed he was winding her up. She might have argued with him and told him he was condescending, that he didn't even know her. She was embarrassed to find that she was mostly angry that their effortless flirting had been disrupted.

Another message from him arrived: 'This meme sums up what I'm talking about'.

A screenshot of a meme followed. It pictured a thin, beautiful white woman with long, dark hair wearing black-framed glasses, a beanie hat, an oversized shirt and a miniskirt. She was slouching with one hand on her hip. She had her chin cocked to the side, defiantly. She looked like a caricature of a cool, sexy, indie girl. She looked like she was trying to be so many things and became ridiculous in the process. The text of the meme read 'I'm not like other girls, I'm into Marvel comics'. He followed this with a laughing emoji, then a kissing emoji.

He thinks I'm contrived, Diane thought. She knew her disappointment was inordinate. She hadn't even met him. He hadn't even asked her out, so this was not a huge loss. She didn't reply but instead took a screenshot of the message and sent it to her friend Rita, who replied 'Red flag number one'. She also sent a green-faced puking emoji. Diane was in the middle of agreeing when she got a notification that Rory had messaged her again.

'Maybe we could meet up and talk about wrestling over

a drink? I can explain to you why WWE is superior to New Japan', it read.

He doesn't know how to be charming, she thought. She went to reply and stopped herself. By that stage, she was in bed, holding the phone above her face. She would luxuriate in withholding a reply until the morning.

She woke up to another message from him.

'Can you stop playing hard to get and meet me for a drink?'

She replied, 'I'm not free until Friday'.

She would cede only so much, as much a compromise with herself as with him. He replied with an emoji that had red love hearts for eyes.

*

In the days before meeting, they continued to message each other constantly.

'I'm looking forward to meeting my pen pal', she told him, the night before their date.

'Do you do this kind of thing often?'

'What kind of thing?'

'Meeting people off dating apps'.

She had met five men, three of whom had never contacted her again. One showed a vague interest but she wasn't attracted to him. Another she dated for about six weeks. He slept over in her house once. She didn't hear from him again afterwards.

She lied and told Rory that she had met two guys through Tinder, so he wouldn't think that she was defective, but that nothing had come of either date.

'Why do you ask?' she replied.

It took him longer than usual to respond. 'No reason. I was just wondering'.

Then: 'I just find that you can never tell what expectations people have'.

She took a screenshot of the conversation again and sent it to Rita: 'What do you think he means by this?'

'Maybe he thinks you're only after one thing', Rita replied.

Diane sent an emoji of a monkey covering its eyes.

Rita then suggested he might be nervous. The idea of him being nervous relieved Diane but also made her pity him in a slightly unpleasant way. She preferred to think of him as self-assured. Realising this made her acknowledge her own anxiety about the date. She resolved to be very kind to him when they met.

*

Rory was shorter than she expected. In his photos he wore glasses but not in person. Without them, the skin around his nose and eyes looked slightly inflamed. He was still very attractive. His teeth were clean and even. His voice was softer than what Diane had imagined. She couldn't imagine him saying anything derisive about her interests in that voice.

Once they got a table in a pub, he asked her what she was drinking. She told him white wine. Whoever had designed the bar had favoured sparse and austere decor. The steel table they sat at was bare apart from a fat, misshapen candle. Dim bulbs hung from the ceiling without any lightshades. The price list for drinks made her feel guilty and anxious all at once.

They talked as easily and as quickly in person as they did online. She imagined getting to meet him in more casual circumstances, at a later stage when it wouldn't require such organisation. Rory was twenty-seven, five years older than her. She was inexplicably impressed by this age gap. If they were actually together, she would like to mention it in conversations with other people. She watched him tear away the label from his beer bottle and imagined being a part of his life.

Rory worked in finance. He liked the work but was frustrated by his colleagues' cynicism and his clients' lack of patience. He complained that it was difficult to progress in his company. He felt stuck in his job and in Dublin, where most of his income was used for rent. But the lack of accommodation made him afraid to leave, afraid he would hate it anywhere else and come back to find that he had nowhere to live.

Diane nodded intently.

He explained that he had started seeing a life coach to help him figure out what step to take next in his career.

Diane was involuntarily horrified by this. She imagined him reciting a *mantra*, asking the universe to help him manifest his *goals*. He continued on, unselfconsciously. Diane criticised herself for being childish and intolerant. You had to see a counsellor when your piano teacher died, she reminded herself.

'I heard that 10 per cent of people working in finance are psychopaths,' Diane said, to change the subject.

He seemed amused by her comment. 'Do you think I'm a psychopath?'

She tilted her head and pretended to consider him.

'I don't think you're a psychopath but you are little bit strange.' A bead of water ran down the side of her wine glass. She caught it with her finger and burst it before it reached the stem. 'You're difficult to read.'

'Am I? What are you trying to determine?' he asked.

She forgot that they hadn't addressed him ridiculing her for her interest in wrestling. 'Well, one moment we're having a laugh and seem to be on the same page. The next you're implying that I pretend to like wrestling or certain music or films in order to impress you. It's offensive.'

He bit his lip and laughed, as if slightly embarrassed. 'Yeah,' he exhaled, 'sorry about that. I don't think about what I'm saying, it's just automatic.'

He unfolded his hands and took hers. 'I like you though.'

She rolled her eyes, as if she believed this were an unnecessary exchange, which was the opposite of how she felt. 'Well, I like you too,' she shrugged, with false indifference.

Even then, she saw their conversation as lukewarm, as not wholly challenging. If he were a friend, she'd categorise him as a boring one. But because they found one another attractive, there was the same generosity that would be applied to a dialogue between two people who did not share the same language. They drank more and moved on to a livelier pub. They became giddy and familiar with each other. They kissed inside the pub, in the smoking area and back out on the street when the pub closed, unaware of anything else.

Her hands were around his neck. His slid down her waist.

'I don't want to let you go home,' he said.

She didn't want to risk assuming he was asking her to go back to his. It would be too embarrassing if she was wrong. To play it safe, she said, 'I know, me too.'

He looked around him, as if considering options. 'I mean, we *could* just go to mine? It's not far. And it's not a school night.'

She feigned hesitation. 'Sure,' she said, 'that would be fine.'

On the way back to his, she observed him chatting and laughing with the taxi driver. He reached across and held her knee, without looking at her and without pausing mid-sentence. She felt excited to be going home with him. But her excitement was so close to apprehension that the two feelings were difficult to distinguish.

Rory's house was a lot nicer than hers, even though he had housemates too. 'We've the cleaner to thank for that,' he explained when she commented on it. She felt the age gap grow between them then. She'd expected kissing in the sitting room before carrying on upstairs. Instead, he poured two glasses of water and brought her straight to his room. He gave her a toothbrush and they cleaned their teeth in front of the mirror in his ensuite bathroom, as if they were already the couple she imagined them to be. Diane tried to sustain the playfulness they had both enjoyed in the bar by pretending to hog the sink and prevent him from spitting out his toothpaste. But Rory ended up dribbling foam down his t-shirt and onto the tiles, which he didn't find funny. She thought he seemed a little angry. Diane needed to use the toilet so she closed the bathroom door. She wondered what he was thinking about during this brief separation.

There were tasteful framed prints hanging on his bedroom wall. On the single shelf above his desk was a small stack of books. They were too neatly arranged to be anything other than ornamental. There were also three green pincushion cacti. They struck her as ugly but fashionable. She was touched when she saw that beside them were two small wrestling figures, both frozen in defensive positions, braced for an attack that they were complicit in.

It was not as easy as she had expected. Their earlier eagerness had been tempered by tiredness and sobriety. They bumped noses and teeth. Diane tried to press into him but he hardened his body to her so she could not slot against him. There were interstitial spaces between them that she failed to close; this she believed to be their problem here.

He preferred to have sex with her while she was facing down. They spent a long time doing it this way and he kept having to pause to catch his breath. She wondered should she ask him to stop but she worried that then it would be obvious that she wasn't enjoying herself. As he entered her, she released a short gasp, for his benefit. When he thrust in and out, she moaned, as if it felt very good. It didn't feel like anything other than addition and then reduction, again and again. She remembered being told that cats only meow in the presence of humans. She thought about meowing during sex and how that might affect him.

*

The following morning it was raining. He made her a coffee and when she was half way through it, he ordered a taxi on his phone. While they waited for it to arrive, he left her alone in the hallway to go look for an umbrella in the utility room. He joined her again, holding a polka-dot umbrella. He looked at his phone.

'The taxi is just outside there.'

Diane wound her scarf around her neck once more.

'Okay, thanks for that.'

She went to hug him. He caught her by her shoulders and kissed her forehead.

*

The sex hadn't been physically enjoyable but she took her own pleasure in thinking about it afterwards: when she arrived home, while she showered, ate and then lay down to sleep for a few hours.

When she woke in the afternoon, she was disappointed to see he hadn't been in touch. She continued to check her phone frequently to look at his WhatsApp status and when he'd last seen his messages. By the time it was dark, she still hadn't heard anything. She had eaten too much that evening, as she was prone to do when hungover or nervous. She felt a vague but diffuse panic every time she looked at her phone.

Diane went to bed that night rigid and unable to sleep.

She decided that if he didn't get in touch by lunchtime the next day, she would contact him.

At noon on Sunday, she messaged Rory to thank him for having her. She was excessively polite, in an effort to be funny.

He replied, saying, 'No problem, it was cool'. He also sent a smiley face.

Nothing in his message indicated that he expected her to reply but she did anyway.

'Yeah, I really enjoyed getting to meet you. I had a really good time'.

He sent another smiley face. She didn't respond.

*

Two months later, the Saturday before Christmas, she woke up to a message he had sent her in the middle of the night. He'd asked her if she was nearby and wanted to meet up. She knew he had sent it while drunk, and, if he remembered doing it, he probably regretted it. Despite this, she was involuntarily elated. When Diane told Rita that Rory had never attempted to arrange a second date, Rita had been kind enough to attribute this to a defect on his part. She'd criticised him harshly, applying standards of romantic conduct that neither she nor Diane had always adhered to in the past. They'd talked at length about the reasons for this quiet rejection, each one more unlikely and speculative than the last. The one that made the least sense but was the most flattering was Rory's potential sense of inadequacy. He could be terrified of being with someone he genuinely likes, Rita concluded. Neither had acknowledged that the most likely reason he did not contact her again also happened to be the least complex: he'd liked her enough to have sex with but not so much to warrant any sort of commitment. Diane pretended to be good natured about it, as if the abruptness of it all could not be helped and was simply to be expected. But as soon as he contacted her again, these spurious feelings of indifference dissipated, as things of poor integrity tend to when tested.

Diane waited until the afternoon to reply to his message. She drafted, deleted and rewrote the reply over and over, deciding it best to be friendly but detached to begin with and eventually sent: 'have you a sore head today?' She threw her phone under a cushion on the couch and busied herself upstairs. In an effort to distract herself, she made ineffectual attempts at tidying her room – she straightened stacks of books and tossed make-up brushes into a drawer but ignored the cups of cold coffee and piles of unwashed clothes. She returned downstairs and boiled the kettle to make tea that she did not drink. She leaned against the counter and scratched nail polish from her fingernails and rearranged the fridge magnets. A bizarre and self-inflicted rule required her to wait one hour before checking her phone. When she did, she was angry to see a message from Rita. They had made vague plans to see a film that night. Diane was no longer interested. She was in the middle of replying when another message came through, from Rory.

'I completely forgot I had messaged you until you texted there!'

Diane replied immediately: 'No way! Were you in a bad way?'

A few minutes later, he responded. 'I'm glad you weren't out last night. I wouldn't have been any use to you if we had crossed paths'.

She typed back, 'Why do you assume I would have met you at all?'

Rory's reply read 'Didn't we have a great night the last time?'

This encouraged her. 'Meeting you in the middle of the night to get a taxi home together isn't how I pictured our second date'.

She could see he had read her message. His status changed from *online* to *typing*. She stared adamantly at the screen. He kept pausing before typing again but no message arrived. After a few moments, he went offline. She ended up going to the cinema with Rita that evening but kept checking her phone surreptitiously. He had been online frequently. Diane knew he had lost interest, like a cat, unmoved by obligation or loyalty, having found a more fulfilling source of pleasure elsewhere.

The next day, she decided to give him a final opportunity, failing to notice he had not sought one. In her message, she told him that she was confused and hurt by how he had treated her. If you're only looking for a drunken hook-up, please don't contact me again. Her tone was short and formal. She hoped to make him feel guilty and embarrassed, but failed abjectly.

'I never said I was after anything serious', he replied. 'I thought you enjoyed yourself so it's a shame that you feel hard done by'.

She knew then that he felt bad but not in a way that might benefit her.

'I didn't enjoy you asking for drunken sex and then ignoring me'.

'If you're looking for more than a one-night stand, don't go home with someone on the first date'.

While Diane's messages were considered, his were written with the carelessness of someone with nothing to lose. The most frustrating thing was how impotent her anger was. Despite her embarrassment, she took a screenshot of the messages and sent them to Rita along with a brief explanation. Rita told her to block him. Diane ignored her message. The whole thing was horrible but it compelled her and she didn't want it to stop.

She replied to Rory: 'I had to shell out forty euro on the morning-after pill because of you'.

This was a lie.

'Sorry you wasted your money', he wrote. 'You must have had too much to drink that night because there was absolutely no need for that'.

'I was sick for the entire weekend', she typed. 'I ended up with a urinary tract infection'.

He replied, 'Then why were you so bothered that I didn't want to see you again?'

'Don't contact me again', she said. Then she messaged him to say that he should be more careful with other people. He did not reply.

'And delete my number', she typed.

For the rest of the day, she felt aimless and disappointed.

She blocked him on WhatsApp and Tinder and Instagram, even though he did not follow her. She deleted his number and cleared all his messages from her phone. Still, she was left unsatisfied. All the preventive measures she had taken were futile and unnecessary: it was unlikely that Rory would ever learn of them.

Arrivals

I don't hear anything for three days, and then on Tuesday night, at the end of my shift at the restaurant, Dan leaves me two WhatsApp voice notes. One is four and a half minutes long and the next is a little over two minutes. He also sends three messages on Instagram (two *Reductress* headlines and a meme about old people on Facebook). It's almost midnight for me, so seven in the evening for him. I play his voice note while cycling home.

'I have had a *truly* awful day,' he begins.

He has been living in New York for seven months and now uses '*truly*' an unnatural amount in conversation. I think he's picked this up from his American friends. But who am I to talk? Until recently I was certain that 'amn't' was a real word, and I often say 'pacifically' instead of 'specifically'. Anyway, I am too critical of people who adopt the accent of the country that they're temporarily living in, as if it isn't normal or healthy for people to change depending on who they spend time with. I start the voice note from the beginning because I wasn't actually listening; my mind had wandered.

'I have had a *truly* awful day. This morning, I was on the train and a couple started a flash mob – actually, maybe it wasn't a flash mob, there was only the two of them, swinging around the poles and twirling around the carriage – but anyway, they caused this huge distraction and everyone was clapping and cheering and I just wanted to listen to 'Picture of You' by Boyzone but couldn't hear it over the commotion. Then I started to think how great it would be if *I* could dance and if people clapped for *me*. So, then I had this fantasy about me competing in one of those *Strictly Come Dancing* charity shows. You know the ones that the local GAA clubs organise as their annual fundraiser? And that's a pathetic ambition but I'm too old to ever be a real dancer so I have to adjust my fantasies to meet my current potential. Because, what's the point in a fantasy if there's no hope it will ever materialise?'

I let out a sloppy laugh, which must seem unbidden to the young couple I cycle past in the dark. I feel bad: I don't have a bike light, and I'm sure that's annoying for drivers and pedestrians. My boyfriend James thinks I replaced my broken light weeks ago, but I keep forgetting and it's a strange lie that I keep telling because I'm embarrassed that I can't reliably complete simple tasks. There are still several minutes of Dan's voice note left.

'Also, I met Paul on my lunch break, and I don't know what's going on there. I told him how upset I was that he ignored me for a week and that I couldn't be with someone who thought that was acceptable behaviour.'

As I'm listening, it's not lost on me that Dan routinely ignores me for a week. The extended silences are followed by lengthy messages, detailed stories of co-workers who have wronged him, run-ins with vaguely famous people or parties that leave him hoarse for days, all the reasons he's been so busy. Lately, I feel like I'm watching him spin on a merry-go-round, at increasing speed, only catching glimpses of him as he passes by. Sometimes, I try to ignore his messages too, to feel as if my life is equally hectic and demanding. But I can rarely last longer than a day. I want to hear what's going on, what he's feeling and thinking.

'Of course, I didn't expect him to *agree*,' he continues. 'He said that he didn't think we should keep seeing each other because he didn't want to hurt me. He said he *cared* about me. Obviously, I started to backtrack then because I was only trying to scare him and the last thing I wanted was for him to call my bluff. And he was so *sad*, saying he had felt really good about us, so then I felt like I had made a *huge* mistake and was almost crying on my way back to the office. But listen, an hour later he texted to say he didn't think he could stop seeing me and invited me to his apartment tonight? So, honestly, I'd say he's full of shit but I'm still really attracted to him so I probably will have sex with him later.'

In the second voice note, he says he got a new job. He doesn't say exactly what it is, but it must be decent if he quit his job as a studio assistant in Bushwick. In the final minute of his message, he tells me that he'll have two weeks off before he starts and that he's decided to visit home this weekend.

I still have a bell on my bike, and ring it four or five times, in excitement. I begin to record a reply, steering with one hand.

'How long are you home for? Will you stay with me while you're here?'

The bike swerves and wobbles, almost colliding with the side of a taxi. The driver lifts a hand in impatience and I straighten up, feeling chastened.

James is still up when I get home. Dan and I moved into this house when we started in NCAD together, seven years ago. After Dan left, James moved in with me. The house belongs to Dan's great-aunt. She lives in a nursing home. We pay a tiny amount of rent to Dan's father. In return, we have to preserve the décor, which includes a lot of framed Sacred Hearts and images of baby Christ and tiny mounted figures depicting his waxy, flushed face and thick lashes as he hangs on the cross, dying. I love it because I'm in the middle of a master's in fine art and find these items an endless source of inspiration for my projects. It's no different to collecting vintage teacups, but James doesn't like it. He's Protestant, although he says it's nothing to do with that: he's asthmatic and the ornaments tend to gather a lot of dust.

James is watching *The Sopranos* when I get home. He abruptly turns off the TV because he's not supposed to watch ahead without me. I lean down and hug him around his neck.

'Colleen, you stink of garlic mayonnaise, it's turning my stomach,' he says, shaking me off.

I catch sight of my reflection in the smudged mirror

across the room. My hair looks matted and my face shiny and red. It surprises me, that inside I can feel so light and yet this is what I look like. I turn away, moving out of sight of the mirror. Fleetingly, I feel irritated with James, as if it's his presence that alters my appearance, making me look unfairly dishevelled.

'Why are you so edgy?' he asks, his eyes following mine as I move through the kitchen.

'Because Dan is coming home next week!' I do a little cancan dance and clap my hands under my leg as it flies mid-air.

'Next week?' James asks, trying to grab my leg.

'Yeah, on Sunday, actually,' I tell him. 'I've asked him to stay here while he's home.'

'Right, absolutely. It's his house. I might stay with Noel while he's here though,' he says.

James and Dan are wary of each other, which is nice for me: I can always complain about one to the other. The only time it has boiled over into outright animosity was at our graduation when James wore a pink velvet jacket with black silk lining. Dan asked James, in front of my parents, if he also smoked one of those novelty bubble-pipes, and shortly afterwards, James slipped the coat off. I think the fact that he'd paid nearly three hundred euro for it made it worse for him.

I sit on the kitchen counter and text Dan again: 'You will stay here though, yes? James won't be around'.

James is still talking and then saying 'Colleen, Colleen, Colleen' in a monotone voice until I shout at him to stop. Dan replies: 'Offended you felt the need to ask. Obviously,

I will be staying with you. I lived there first'. James accuses me of not listening to him until I insist that I *am* listening, and ask can he just repeat the last bit.

*

On Wednesday, I have class all day. After finishing my degree, I worked for two years in a small gallery before deciding to go back for my master's. I only did this because Dan had found a job in New York, a revelation which made me feel betrayed: I had thought we were both supposed to be flailing, stumbling and floundering our way through together. I had known he was more talented than me, but I didn't think he cared about that. So, I panicked and now I owe the credit union eight thousand euros.

My class is arranging an exhibition of all our work for January. My classmate, Nathaniel, is especially versatile and if he were a woman, I'd feel threatened by this. He makes a lot of art about climate change and the futility of our efforts to mitigate its effects. He created an artificial river in a block of concrete and will invite participants to deposit their litter in the river, until it chokes the flow and cuts off the water. Nathaniel is also the best in our class at digital design. I'm struggling with Adobe Illustrator, so I ask him to help me after class. James is a graphic designer so I could go to him, but I don't because I like spending time with Nathaniel.

'Oh yeah, I see what you've done wrong: you've tried to place this image as a jpeg, but you should load it in Photoshop first, then resize it,' he tells me, after I present him with a problem I could have googled. He could have told me to google it, but he didn't.

I don't know when I got so fickle. I think it's because I don't believe I'm attractive. So, even if James likes how I look, it's not enough reassurance. At an initial glance, I have a well-proportioned body and nice red hair. But my eyes are a little too close together and my nose is small and round and my philtrum is a little too long so I sometimes think I look like a gnome. And my neck is too short, Dan always says this. It's terrible for a woman to have no neck, it just is.

Nathaniel walks up Thomas Street with me, until I get to work. He says he's been invited to speak at the National Gallery about a piece of his they've selected for a themed exhibition. I ask him questions and hardly listen to the answers, focusing too much on the next piece of insight I can offer. He's talking to me about the end of the world, how it's already happening and that we shouldn't really think of it as one final event but as a series of increasingly devastating disasters.

He's not looking at me as I reply, but he's bent his head ever so slightly so that his ear is cocked closer to me, as he nods slowly while I talk about the ethics of having children, using that voice that James always calls contrived. He never said things like that in the early days. It's only in the past year that he's started to criticise me for silly, inconsequential remarks, things I don't even mean. Well, he's probably right. The idea of not having children – it's baseless, really, and would surely crumble under scrutiny. But Nathaniel doesn't prod too much, because I suspect he likes his interlocutors to be as intelligent as he is, even if it's an artificial projection. We walk like that, so slowly that we start to bump shoulders. Every so often, we stop altogether, leaning against the brick wall of a café, pressing ourselves closer to allow people to get by. I can hear James criticising me, asking, What are you *doing* Colleen? And I don't know, James, probably just pretending. We carry on like this, making our way slowly to my job at the Greek restaurant. For the whole night, I'm having conversations in my head, one with Nathaniel and the other with James. I turn my face side to side, to see what each one might say.

*

'You're going to make a fool of yourself if you keep this up,' Dan says in a voice note when I tell him about this thing with Nathaniel. 'You're bored, so what? Grow up.'

This is Friday. I know he can't find his passport so he's taking it out on me. But, to be fair, he's always surprisingly loyal to James. Last year, when James was unemployed and depressed, he started doing creepy things like playing Édith Piaf in the bath and secretly reading my emails. When I told Dan, he was excessively kind, insisting that James needed my support and understanding, not judgement. I resented him scolding me. It was embarrassing, as if I didn't know right from wrong and needed to be told.

'Obviously, I was never going to do anything,' I start to reply. I end up recording the message and deleting it three times, suddenly annoyed, with myself and with him. He does this all the time. I'll think we're both on the same page, scandalised and amazed by the turn of events in our lives. But then I'll find out he's not sharing the same experience as me, that we weren't even talking about his experience to begin with.

On Saturday, I wait in arrivals and see Dan before he sees me. He's walking with a travel cushion around his neck and looks a little irritated, as if he thinks I'm late. I start to laugh because I can see him mouth 'For God's sake' and start to call me on his phone. I get right up next to him, before he even realises it's me. There's a moment when he hesitates and I know that if I don't wrap my arms around his shoulders, we'll waste too much time feeling like we don't know each other so well anymore.

It takes us over an hour to get back because I can't remember where I parked the car. I've made a lasagne, and we watch three episodes of *Buffy* and then when the wine is gone, we go to the off-licence for more. Then we come home to watch *Muriel's Wedding*, but Dan falls asleep halfway through. When I get a message from Nathaniel, I mute the television.

'Colleen!' he writes. Friendly. 'A few of us are going to Lucky's tomorrow. You up for it?'

I draft my reply in the notes app on my phone before committing to typing anything in WhatsApp: 'Nathaniel! Class, love Lucky's! My friend's home from New York and staying with me, so if he's up for it, we'll see you there!' I delete the second exclamation mark and add a smiley, then get rid of that too.

I watch the status under his name change from *online* to *typing* for a few moments until I'm startled by Dan, who wakes himself up with an abruptly loud snore. I guide him upstairs and he sleeps in my bed, on James's side.

'It's temp work, my new job,' Dan tells me the next morning, as I burn the scrambled eggs. 'I'm just sick of working sixty-hour weeks to support someone else's art. And what's wrong with wanting to work a normal job? What does it matter? Once I can pay my rent, who cares?'

'Did you tell your dad?' I ask.

'Yeah, but I told him it's permanent and that there's opportunity for promotion. He's thrilled.'

He scrapes at an unrecognisable piece of food stuck to the side of his coffee mug with his thumbnail. James never cleans the dishes properly: it's always just this rushed, cursory rinse.

'Actually, never mind anyone else's art, I'm just sick of it in general,' he says. 'I'm sick of this pursuit of originality. It's joyless and it's not as if anyone other than me even cares.'

I plate the eggs and pour us some juice.

'I don't like anything I've made. I'm just looking at it hoping it's more interesting than what everyone else is making. And who am I helping? What am I contributing to the world?' He pauses, looks around. 'Salt?'

I pass it to him.

'It makes you a narcissist, to care this much about art. I know we need it and that people appreciate it.' He looks up at me then. 'I just can't really stand it, at the minute.'

I frown solemnly, as if I feel sorry for him. Privately, I'm ashamed to find I'm relieved. He's as ordinary as I am. Maybe he won't shoot ahead, beyond my reach. He might even move home, and we could revert to our earlier lives, comfortably and predictably average lives.

After I shower, I shout down to Dan that the bathroom's free but he doesn't reply. Back in my room, when I swing my bedroom door shut, he leaps out from behind it, causing me to shriek.

'Jesus Christ, Dan!' I say, grabbing my pillow and smacking him with it. 'You're a child, seriously.'

This shouldn't have been a surprise, not when he used to lie underneath my bed, waiting for me to come into my room and grab my ankle as I walked by. I'd try to catch him out by hiding in his wardrobe, but I wouldn't be able to withhold my stupid laughter for long enough. 'Colleen,' he'd say flatly, 'get out of my room.' As if nothing I did ever affected him.

'Will we go to Lucky's tonight?' I ask him, as we walk along Clontarf seafront with two 99s.

He pulls a face. 'I'll probably go there loads this week, Colleen.'

'The people from my class are going. You might like them.'

'Is Nathan going?' he asks.

'Nathaniel? Maybe.' My wrists are sticky. Chocolate sauce has dribbled down my sleeve.

'Don't pretend you want to show me off. If you want to see him, we'll go,' he says.

I'm annoyed at him for addressing this with such direct calm. It makes me feel foolish, like my behaviour is inevitable and therefore unworthy of disappointment or reprimand.

*

At Lucky's, I spot Nathaniel sitting between two guys at a crowded table. There are no seats available, so, rather than loom over them, Dan and I stand across from his table, at the bar. I turn my face away from him and do my best to focus only on what Dan is saying. His voice trails away for a moment and his eyes focus over my left shoulder. 'If James finds out, he will never forgive you, and I wouldn't blame him,' he says, with a thin smile, before walking away and nodding at Nathaniel, who has come to stand in his place.

We stay so long, it's like we're waiting everyone else out. I start to yawn in Nathaniel's face, I can't help it. Over the course of three hours, I begin to slowly regret this stupid little fantasy. The more he drinks, the more Nathaniel repeats himself, saying over and over, in different ways that, *actually*, you have to wonder how ethical it is to engage in self-care, these days.

'I'm actually considering submitting a piece about it, to the *Times*. About how practices like meditation and yoga are ultimately useless. They have a sedative effect. Certainly, they make people feel better, but they don't actually address any real problem, you know?'

He's rude to the bar staff too. But it's too late now because everyone else is huddled in their own little groups. Dan is locked into an intense-looking conversation with a mature student, a woman with red hair styled in dreadlocks. I have hardly ever spoken to her before. I feel fleetingly jealous that he can commit so fully to his interactions with people. I'd be glancing around me, trying to see if there were more interesting conversations between more impressive people happening elsewhere.

Gradually, people splinter off, the groups growing smaller and smaller as everyone begins to leave. Dan joins us once again, after he's run out of people to talk to.

'That woman, Tanya, with the hair? So interesting! Her partner left her two years ago and now she lives on a boat.' He shakes his head incredulously.

Out on the street, the three of us amble away from the pub. Nathaniel pulls a grey tartan paddy cap out of his coat pocket. I've never seen him wear anything like this before, it's awful looking. Dan walks a few steps ahead of us, unaware that I've had a change of heart. When we find a taxi, Dan pulls the door open and asks Nathaniel if he'd like to come for a drink at ours, perhaps thinking he's doing me some kindness.

'Actually, I was hoping I might be able to sleep on your couch, Colleen, if that's okay?' Nathaniel asks. 'I've forgotten my house keys and I don't think my housemates will be awake at this hour.'

Dan's already in the taxi and I can't catch his eye. I wish he'd tell Nathaniel he can't stay, but of course he doesn't. He doesn't live there anymore, so it's not up to him.

Dan hardly has one drink before he says he's off to bed. I'm staring at him, hoping he'll meet my eyes for long enough to see I need to be rescued from this awful mistake. His gaze glides past mine and he leaves Nathaniel and I alone, on the couch. I stand up and make myself busy at the sink, washing my glass.

'No way, the shrine is a bit much, isn't it?' Nathaniel says.

I turn around and see him stand up to inspect the

glowing Sacred Heart and the collection of religious items surrounding it. He pulls out his phone and starts to record a video.

'I have to put this on my Instagram stories, it's so fucked up,' he laughs.

'They're all Dan's,' I say, stupidly. I won't engage in any sort of analysis with him. I decide to treat him with an opaque, kind courtesy, my answers short and leaden, like a heavy door slamming shut.

He stands over the items, tugging at his lip thoughtfully. I don't want to hear his insight; I don't want to hear any observation he has about what these items say about me or Dan or our culture. In this very moment, I'm disgusted with myself for caring about art and being impressed with someone like Nathaniel and for thinking I can reduce everyone I meet down to whatever it is that makes me pity them, as if people don't already know what their problem is. I don't want to see this man ever again and I wish I could tell him to leave now but the best I can manage is to tell him he can sleep on the couch. He's taken aback, lost for words, at last. I go to bed and I cry, which is ridiculous, but I call James and I tell him that I brought a friend home and that I feel terrible. I don't say anything about how much I pushed and orchestrated this because it would be too awful. I need him to know what happened but not why it happened. And he's so kind – he even laughs, and says he knows he can always trust me because I feel guilty about the silliest things.

*

I wake up after ten and creep down the stairs. There's nothing left on the couch except a crumpled-up blanket. I climb back upstairs and pause at Dan's room. I open the bedroom door carefully. He's still asleep. I get a sudden urge to laugh and cover my mouth with my palm. How much longer can he sleep? I get on my hands and knees and slide my body under his bed. I lie on my stomach, my face against the carpet. If I can wait long enough, I might just be able to grab his ankle as he gets out of bed. Forget about desire, it gives me such pleasure, to imagine catching him out like that.

Settling Down

The man appeared huge in their apartment door, filling the entire frame of it. He had full, sallow cheeks and coarse black hair, the front of which fell across his forehead, curling and wet. His sturdiness made the furniture in Cliona and Ben's apartment appear flimsy, the cheap paintings and vases a failed attempt to hide the shabbiness of the carpet and curtains, things they couldn't really afford to replace.

He introduced himself as Leo, shaking their hands. He called Cliona 'young lady' and Ben 'sir'. In neither case did it strike Cliona as patronising or deferential, and she wondered how he did that. His work trousers were wide and at the end of his legs were feet that were surprisingly small. It gave the impression of a stocky man sitting on an adolescent's shoulders, poorly disguising the arrangement with a long coat.

Cliona guided him through to the bathroom, where she switched on a light to illuminate what looked like several cups of wet coffee grounds thrown against the walls. Leo gasped as he stepped around Ben and Cliona and into their dim and narrow bathroom. The mould was dense and textured in the corners of the ceiling. As it spread toward the shower and toilet, it grew expansive and speckled. The air was humid. It had rained constantly for two days, which had only made things worse. The walls in every room were wet to touch and the paint had started to swell and blister.

Leo rubbed a hand across his stubble. 'I've been doing this for decades, but I think this could be the worst I've ever seen.' Only then did Cliona detect a slight South African accent.

Leo turned around, and as he looked into the kitchen, his face grew almost sorrowful to see the mould had spread there too. 'Oh, would you look at the state of that. It's like a Victorian hospital,' he tutted, stretching his hand towards it.

'The landlord said it's because we spend too much time at home,' Cliona ventured.

Ben chimed in then, apparently encouraged by her lead. 'Yeah, he said that our breath causes too much condensation and the ventilation system can't handle it.'

'Oh, how inconsiderate of you,' Leo said dryly. He stepped across the hall into the kitchen. '*Breathing* in your own home.' He reached up to pull away the slotted cover of what appeared to be an air extractor. Behind it was nothing but a narrow hole. 'I suppose you cook here too. In the place you pay rent to live? The nerve.' He chuckled, crossing his eyes, severely, as if dumbfounded by the idea.

Ben laughed, slowly. He liked expressive people, especially when it came as a surprise.

This was the second damp expert the landlord had sent out. The first man had obviously been instructed by him to insist it wasn't all that unusual to find mould growing on your clothes or shoes. It was an old building, what did they expect? Cliona had been defeated and wanted to let it go, but after several chest and ear infections, the landlord eventually agreed to send a second expert to them.

On the phone, Cliona had heard Ben say, 'A real one this time, not one of your friends you're paying to fob us off.' She had been washing up after dinner in the kitchen and the remark made her press a soapy hand to her mouth.

Ben wore his sleek, brown hair in a ponytail and had long lashes and dark, watery eyes. This belied a temerity that made Cliona both nervous and proud. She worried that he would be too strident in his complaints, that they might be evicted. This apartment was good value, with a large bedroom and a separate kitchen and sitting room. They could hardly afford a studio elsewhere for the same rent. When she voiced this fear, Ben criticised her weakness. They'd be alright, he insisted. How though? She pressed. They had already been looking elsewhere and they couldn't even get a viewing. She knew he didn't have a plan, just the assurance that he could go back to his parents. Meanwhile, her brother, his girlfriend and their daughter took over her parents' place. It hurt that he didn't seem to consider this.

'I understand that you are planning to pay half the cost while the landlord will pay the rest, yes?' Leo asked, then.

Ben rolled his eyes, reluctantly agreed. This of course had been another point of contention, something Ben was bitter about capitulating to.

'I'll get a quote across to you this afternoon,' said Leo. 'I imagine it should come in around twelve hundred,' he said tentatively.

'So, we'd pay six hundred, then,' Ben said.

Although he appeared causal, she knew Ben was relieved. Between them they could afford no more than eight hundred. Even then, this expense would use up nearly all of her rainy-day fund. He was a German teacher who also taught classical guitar at the weekend. She had worked briefly in an advertising agency, an enervating yet hectic role she'd hated. In confusion and desperation, Cliona had believed she might be too creative for the job. Not once did it occur to her that she might be too stupid. Now she worked in customer service for a medical supply company and loved it. But their combined salary didn't amount to much. They split everything as evenly as possible and whatever disposable income left was spent with guilt and care.

Although it appeared that Leo's survey of the apartment was complete, he lingered for another fifteen minutes, listening to their complaints of how the mould had affected their life and belongings. It was hard to know when they ought to hold back, whether they might appear ungrateful, if Leo might privately consider them precious. But his shock at their problem was too gratifying to leave alone. They showed him the green and furry mould that had taken hold of their photo frames, the damp that had weakened their mahogany desk and the puddles of water pooling around the window frames. Just wait, they said, see for yourself. If you just follow us through here, it gets so much worse.

After he left, both Cliona and Ben were reinvigorated. There was housework to be done, but theirs was the pent up, unfocused sort of energy that comes with feeling vindicated, so they decided to take a walk instead. It was a wet evening but mild and still bright. In the park near their apartment, the trees were silvery and moist, the branches stark but heavy with nascent unfurling leaves. They both tried not to talk about the mould; it was too dreary to obsess over. But invariably they found the conversation looping back around to Leo. When they ran out of things to say, one would turn to the other and cross their eyes in imitation of Leo in the kitchen. Wasn't he a decent sort of person, Ben insisted. A decent *country* sort of person, Cliona, who had grown up in West Clare, added. Yes, they agreed. It was hard to come by, sometimes. It was nice, for a change.

*

Cliona was forced to take the morning off work for Leo's next visit. Ben would be in school, teaching until half three. The idea of being alone with Leo made her nervous, not because she felt threatened but because she feared Ben's absence would make her less inhibited. She worried she might ramble inanely, a nervous habit Ben had identified five years earlier when they first got together. It was then a relief that Leo arrived with two other men, a broad-shouldered young man and an older, soft-spoken man who immediately asked to use the bathroom, the request urgent and anxious. He had small eyes with large, dark irises. He also addressed Cliona as 'ma'am'. Her amusement at this seemed to perplex him, which she felt bad about.

At first, Leo delayed telling her what they were about to do, asking if she ought to take notes to relay to Ben, later on. He then seemed impressed by her insistence that this was unnecessary, she would understand. Even in the moment, the triumph of winning his approval was a little unpleasant. It was like this sometimes, with men. She had the feeling of being a scurrying rodent, vying for the little piece of cheese or bread from the man's hand. Yes, you're happy to be fed but you're still just a mouse.

First, they would install an extractor fan in the bathroom. Cliona lingered, unsure whether she would need to be consulted. It quickly became clear that the younger man was aggrieved to be taking orders from Leo. He interrupted him several times, contradicting his instructions, suggesting they use a different method to the one Leo had decided. At first, Leo was patient, allowing that, yes, in theory that method was perfectly suitable, but that in his experience, his *considerable* experience, it just wasn't quite as effective as his own.

Only when the younger man grew openly frustrated did Leo employ a sharper tone. He instructed the younger man to retrieve a tool, but he could not find it. He had emptied the boxes of equipment and was certain it wasn't there. He swivelled around, gesturing to the floor, insistent that Leo had forgotten it. There were several tools and pieces of equipment that Cliona could not identify on the carpet, as well as lengths of white plastic tubing. The younger man's voice grew slightly irate. There wouldn't be time to drive back to get it — they had another job at two o'clock. What were they supposed to do?

Leo surveyed the equipment slowly, before pointing to the man's left foot, at something that looked to Cliona like a large, rusted eyelash curler.

'Well, what's that, at your feet then, ah?' he asked. 'What would you call that? A cream bun?' He looked at the older man then, who chuckled obediently.

'Yeah,' the older man added quietly, knowing whom to align himself with, 'it's his lunch, I'd say.'

The younger man bent to pick up the item in question, his face red. It appeared he had taken it from the box, hadn't recognised it for what it was and discarded it. Cliona pitied him for trying so hard only to come up a fool in the end.

The men worked solidly and noisily for two and a half hours. Cliona offered them tea or coffee, but Leo refused, frowning as if a hot drink would be premature and uncouth. They had managed to install extractor fans in the bathroom and kitchen but would need to schedule another visit to install a ventilation unit in the bedroom. Leo invited Cliona to the bathroom, to see how the fan worked. She hovered at the threshold while he stood by the sink. The bathroom was narrow and cramped. To fit two people in there you would need to close the door.

'Come on in now, young lady,' he said. 'You can close that door. I'm not going to bite.'

Cliona sidled around the door and pushed it shut. The air was close and warm.

'Now, I'm going to ask you to turn on your shower for me there,' he told her.

She followed his instruction and soon steam had risen from the shower. The fan began whirring, rhythmically.

He clapped his hands together. 'Excellent, that's working away for you now, my girl.'

His expression grew mischievous. He pointed an index finger upwards. 'You know, I often say it, I have plenty of women, my *clients*, who claim that when they're in the shower and they hear that fan get going, the first thing they think of is me.'

Cliona couldn't help but laugh too, his was infectious. She'd been subjected to this kind of thing before, being cornered by a man, at a party or in the office, only for him to say something strange to elicit a reaction, fear or disgust. She felt neither. She didn't feel tricked or threatened. It was difficult to fathom, because she wasn't the kind of person to tolerate any innuendo, even if it appeared harmless. Usually, she considered comments adjacent to Leo's as belonging to the broad base of the pyramid of misogyny, behaviour to be stamped out immediately. For the first time, she could empathise with those women who found themselves taken in by a charismatic cult leader.

Leo suddenly appeared thoughtful. 'But Jesus, I mean no offence. You know, I have grandchildren now, I'm too old for that kind of thing.' He lifted his hands, which trembored slightly, as if to dispel the idea. He took his phone from his pocket and flashed a screensaver photo of two toddlers crouched near a murky pond. Cliona smiled to reassure him, but didn't add to the joke, for fear she might appear coarse and incapable of pulling it off the way he did.

*

That Friday, they met Ben's friend Chris and his new girl-friend Lauren at a rundown but trendy Mexican place on the outskirts of town. The tables were lined with benches and the two couples sat across from each other, squeezed between two other parties, bumping shoulders and elbows. This was how it was: Chris had plenty of money, but he liked these cheap, authentic places and knew an unnatural amount about the owners and their staff, which was sometimes welcome but mostly not.

When Cliona and Ben first met Lauren, she told them she met Chris in a bookshop, could they believe that? They raised their eyebrows and drew back their shoulders, subtle gestures that allowed them to have their own word-less conversation, one they would have verbally once they were alone. They would know exactly what the other was thinking in that moment. What Lauren didn't know is that Chris had first seen her in a café and then followed her to the bookshop, contriving an opportunity to introduce himself.

'How's the black mould situation going?' Chris waggled his eyebrows, looking between Ben and Cliona.

Cliona turned to Lauren. 'We have a bit of a damp issue in our apartment. There's a lot of black mould sprouting up.'

She returned a half-eaten mushroom taco to her plate. 'Ew,' she said softly.

'Yes. It's disgusting,' Cliona said before turning to Chris. 'But we have made progress. The landlord finally sent somebody decent and it looks like we can get it sorted out now.'

When Cliona described Leo's charisma and energy, Ben appeared almost as invested in the story at first. Only when she started to describe his diplomatic approach to dealing with his jealous young employee could she sense him disengage.

'It was nothing to do with ego, you know? He had to put him in his place, but it was for the greater good, so that they could all work together peacefully and with an understanding of the hierarchy.' Even then, she could see Chris and Lauren were bored but she couldn't help herself, she couldn't stop talking about it.

'Tell them what he said to you in the bathroom,' Ben suggested, identifying a more interesting thread of the story.

'Oh yes!' She was happy to describe the interaction. In doing so, she was careful not to exaggerate anything.

'How was it that he could do that without making me feel uncomfortable?' she wondered. 'How did he pull that off?'

'You're one of his *clients*, now,' was all Chris said.

'Wait, who's this again?' Lauren piped up. Cliona had the impression that Lauren really listened only when Chris was speaking. She didn't dislike her for this – she thought it wise. Lauren would need to conserve most of her energy for him if she wanted it to work out.

'Cliona's falling in love with a plumber,' Chris told her. At heart, he was a real snob.

'He's not a plumber, he's a damp expert,' Cliona said.

'But she is falling for him,' Ben added dryly. 'We're considering an open relationship.' He leaned on his elbows and fixed his eyes on Lauren, waiting for her reaction. Cliona had forgotten how much he enjoyed flirting with new women.

'But seriously,' Cliona went on, placing a hand on Ben's wrist to silence him, 'I just think it's interesting, the difference that body language and implied intent make in these situations, don't you?'

She looked at all three of them, noting their clear *lack* of interest. Even Lauren gave nothing more than a polite nod. Cliona felt like she was talking about a long-running but failing research project, a specialised interest no one else cared about.

She also knew she was veering close to Ben's least favourite topic: the silent conversation between men and women, the daily subtle but pervasive line of communication that varied from lustful to patronising, from insistent to violent. She experienced this almost only with straight men, largely because there was no apparent need for any subterranean conversation with other people. It was fleeting and impossible to prove, yet she allowed it to inform and define the entire interaction. This silent conversation could even be quite intimate, and, depending on its extent, this intimacy could create greater distance between her and the man on the surface, as though they were both ashamed. Sometimes, she perceived impatience and resentment and sometimes she sensed tenderness, affection even. It was the tenderness that confused her and got her into trouble. It led her to obsess over the man and create expansive and improbable stories about him in her head. This was the thing that Ben disliked. Ben didn't day-dream. He took everything at face value. He never let his instinct overcome the bare facts of the situation.

The more Cliona drank, the harder she found it to stop talking about Leo. Even as they ate their ice cream, she found herself prompting Ben, saying things like, 'But isn't he wasted in his day job? Shouldn't he be on stage or television?'

'Doing what?' he asked, no longer willing to be complicit.

'I don't know,' she said. 'He could negotiate hostage situations. Or host one of those shows where he communicates with the audience's dead relatives.'

At this, Chris snorted: 'Oh, they're all full of shit.'

She shook her head, but knew not to say anything else, at last. Sometimes it was like this: she failed to explain her thoughts properly.

*

It was surreal for her to learn, soon after, that of course Leo wasn't wasted in his day job, that he had a full life besides that. Cliona discovered through googling his name, while drunk after the dinner with Chris and Lauren, that he also ran a charity, a stream of counselling services that ranged from addiction support groups to marriage media-tion. The website included a biography that was lengthy and personal. His daughter's life had been ravaged by addiction and mental illness. She eventually recovered as an adult, but as Leo noted, there were few supports for her, or their family, something that he believed hindered the healing process. He'd found help from community groups, resources he felt were underfunded. In his early fifties, he retrained as a counsellor (it tugged at Cliona's heart to imagine him as a mature student, earnest and nervous). Alongside two other therapists, one who specialised in bereaved adolescents and another in trauma and crisis management, he ran his services out of a renovated parish hall. Why hadn't she thought of looking him up earlier? Possibly because she felt embarrassed by the extent of her fascination with him while sober.

*

It was the following Saturday before Leo returned, this time alone, to install the final ventilation unit in their bedroom. Because Cliona was now slightly more familiar with him than Ben was, she could feel the plane of their dynamic tilting, so that much of the conversation darted back and forth between her and Leo. Leo tried to include Ben, by praising his perseverance with the landlord, saying that a man like that just wants to make as much money as possible, that's all he cares about. Ben only shrugged, his dark eyes indifferent and remote.

Leo began heaving the unit through the sitting room and into their bedroom, one leg dragging slightly behind the other, leaving muddy smears on their linoleum. Cliona mouthed to Ben: 'Help. Him.'

'Do you need a hand with anything, Leo?' Ben called into the bedroom.

'No, no, I have everything here now,' he replied, breathless.

Ben turned around and angled his face to Cliona, as if to say, Happy now?

It took Leo less than forty-five minutes to finish the job. The bedroom carpet was coated in flakes of paint and chips of wood. He told them that once they painted over the mould, it shouldn't return. This time, when Cliona offered him a cup of tea, he accepted it. In the kitchen, Leo pulled out a chair from under the table and sat down. Cliona leaned against counter while Ben hovered near the door frame.

After an extended silence, Leo cleared his throat. 'If you don't mind, I'm about to pay you both a compliment,' he began carefully. 'I can tell, from the limited time I've had with you both in the last couple of weeks, that the communication between you is strong.' He made a fist with his free hand.

He looked towards the fogged-up window. 'I'm killed telling people this, really, but the line of communication between a couple is the backbone of a relationship. It has to be clear, and it has to be mutual.' He took a loud gulp from his cup and turned back towards them, shrugging modestly. 'I moonlight as a counsellor. I only do it part-time, but I do have some idea what I'm talking about.'

Ben's laughter was abrupt and incredulous.

'I know,' Leo said, calmly. 'You wouldn't think it, looking at me.' He gestured to his frayed work trousers and scuffed boots. Leo sat back and squinted. 'I mean, I work with couples – mediation, reconciliation – and the people I help, it's really only a 50 per cent success rate. It all depends on what they want to do, obviously.

'But I have a good feeling about you two,' he went on. 'There's just something about the way you are together. It's a quiet sort of thing, but I'd say it works, doesn't it?'

He looked at them expectantly and waited for their confirmation. It came slow and shy. They'd never talked about the quality of their relationship before, only that of those they came in contact with.

'Look,' Leo said blithely, placing the empty cup on the kitchen table. 'You might not think it now, but you'll probably get married and have kids, at some point.'

Noticing Ben's expression changing, Leo regarded him gravely and carried on. 'Believe me, you think it won't happen.' He paused and stood up. 'But it does. And when it does, you'll need each other. You'll need to keep the line of communication open. Remember that – keep it strong and clear.'

He moved to gather the tools he'd brought with him. Both Ben and Cliona walked with him to the elevator, carrying the few things he couldn't manage. Once the chrome doors slid open, he held a boot against it, preventing it from closing prematurely. He looked around a final time at the balding carpet and dented concrete walls. When he spoke, he looked directly at Ben.

'And the next time you move, find her somewhere nicer than this, would you?' He grinned then conspiratorially at Cliona. 'You're not students anymore. If comfort doesn't matter to you now, it will soon.'

They walked silently back to their apartment. Cliona was afraid to say anything in case Leo heard her through the thin walls. Once the lock was turned in the door, Ben pressed one eye to the peephole, to make sure he hadn't come back, having forgotten something.

'What a load of *shite*,' he hissed. 'My head is *wrecked* listening to him. Imagine going to him for counselling. A 50 per cent success rate? What good is that?'

It wasn't necessary for Cliona to respond. He was aggravated, off on a tangent, and didn't require any reinforcement in order to continue.

'Also, anyone could tell you that communication is important. Easily the most clichéd advice I've ever heard about relationships.'

Meanwhile, Cliona wondered why Leo assumed they'd get married and have children. Ben seized up with displeasure whenever she told him about a friend getting pregnant. 'That's their life over' was all he'd say, as though they had received a terminal diagnosis that he'd been lucky enough to avoid. This had seemed like something that might eventually change as they got older. Now, she felt stupid for her earlier hopefulness. Why would he ever change? And they were both thirty-two, almost thirty-three. What was going to happen, exactly? She'd been too afraid to ask, in case she was told that this was the most he was willing to offer. Would they just tumble along, as they had for the last few years, until one of them decided they had enough? She thought about some of her friends with children, whom she had previously believed she pitied. They couldn't up and leave and start a new life at the drop of a hat. But when would she do that either? She didn't even want a new life.

In the hours after Leo left, she began to understand more thoroughly why it was that his assessment had bothered her: he'd been wrong about them as a couple. He'd assumed that they were compatible and equally invested in a shared future, which wasn't true. There was an imbalance that left her with less power. It was disappointing, not simply because it forced her to acknowledge an unhappy truth about her relationship, but also because it made her lose faith in Leo's wisdom.

Surely they would have to talk about this. Ben would start to think about it too when he calmed down, he'd have to. The implications of Leo's advice would start to dawn on him. They couldn't just ignore it and carry on as they had before, wandering aimlessly through life together, only tenuously attached. She took a shower and washed her hair, an activity that helped her in overwhelming moments. The fan began to whir and, yes, she thought of Leo, but it was he who planted the idea in her head. Probably he'd made it up and the only reason he came to anyone's mind in the shower was because he'd already created an earlier association. It was a psychological trick, something difficult to prove either way.

Even after they painted over the mould, it would return. They learned too late that it had nothing to do with the circulation of clean, dry air. The extractor fans and ventilation unit whirred uselessly, driving their electricity bills up but doing nothing to improve the damp conditions. It was the insulation, the single-paned windows, the poor infrastructure. The whole building was riddled with damp, and the only way to fix it would be to tear through the rotted walls and start all over again. They could either learn to live with it or leave. The landlord would find other tenants, poorer than Ben and Cliona, who would be satisfied with a roof over their heads.

The Slip

Colm woke up at eight to the sound of Norma on the landing, running the head of the hoover noisily against the box-room door. He'd slept for only four hours. He was tempted to call in sick again, to turn over and close his eyes for another few hours. But everyone knew this was the worst thing you could do because it only disturbed the sleep pattern further. Either way, he was going to be late to work now. Why couldn't Norma have woken him an hour earlier? He was about to get up when she burst into the room without knocking.

'Oh, *good*,' she said cheerfully, striding over to the window and flinging the curtains open. 'You're awake at last.'

She wore her cleaning clothes: a white cotton t-shirt without a bra and a pair of tracksuit bottoms that looked too small across her thighs. She hadn't brushed her hair or applied any make-up yet and the greyish-purple bags under her eyes made Colm feel nauseous. They reminded him of undercooked bacon fat.

It was a bright Thursday morning in early May. There was a streak of green and white bird shit on the box-room window.

'Oh, wipe that away, would you? Before it dries in.' She tutted.

He went to speak but she was already distracted by some odour in the air. She turned her nose up and sniffed.

'You should leave the window open overnight. There's a bad smell in here in the mornings,' she said, waving her hand in front of her nose. She had complained of his morning smell for as long as they had been together. Norma was gone from the room before he could answer.

Colm hadn't been able to get a decent night of sleep since their sixteen-year-old cat Pogo died. He began sleeping in the box room shortly after, so that his tossing and turning wouldn't wake Norma. The vet had cautioned him that Pogo's prognosis wasn't good, but Colm hadn't wanted to hear it. He'd thrown money at anything that might help keep Pogo comfortable, something Norma coolly remarked was out of character for him. Just as he'd thought they had gotten a handle of Pogo's kidney medicine, just as Colm thought he'd turned a corner, Pogo disappeared late in the evening without returning home. Colm wandered half that night searching for him, to no avail. It wasn't until the next morning, when they let Joey the Labrador out for a whizz, that Colm saw Pogo curled up beneath the rusted sun chair they often shared on milder days.

This loss caused him greater distress than the death of his father, less than a year earlier. Originally bought for their son, Francis, who named the cat Pogo because he was so jumpy at first, the tortoiseshell-coated creature became like a child to Colm, one who never grew up and expected very little in return. With Pogo's stiff body on his lap, Colm wept openly, while Norma hovered over him, gripping his shoulders.

'Poor pet,' she said, stroking Colm's hair.

'Oh, I'll miss him so much, I really will,' he said, leaning down to kiss Pogo's fur.

'We *all* will,' she said solemnly. 'Sixteen years is a long time – it won't be the same.'

Even then, the comment irritated him. Norma had always shooed Pogo off the couch and had ridiculed Colm's affection for him. Why couldn't she allow him this one grievance without intruding on it and trying to claim it as her own?

Later on, when he drove Francis to the library, he said as much to him, unable to let it go.

'She was crying, yes, but there weren't any *tears*. It just looked forced. Do you know what I mean? What do you think?'

Francis only grunted, refusing to agree or disagree, and fiddled with the dial on the radio. Colm should have known better than to rely on his son for reinforcement. It was as if even listening to Colm complain about his mother was a betrayal. It was all so hypocritical. He'd overheard the two of them mock him in the utility room, where Francis often assisted Norma in folding or ironing clothes, plenty of times. Apparently, Colm's clothes were unfashionable and he was too tight with money. At first, it stung him to hear these insults. Despite this, he felt compelled to spy on them. It never seemed to occur to them that he was right there, listening at the other side of the door, straining to hear their whispers.

*

It had been a strange year. Colm's father died and then he had a dental abscess followed by a slipped disc, two of the most physically painful events he could remember. Then, his younger brother was named executor of his father's will instead of Colm. It wasn't that his father had money or that Colm even cared about the distribution of his limited assets. It was just that, in his own way, he was insecure enough to want his father to have had faith that Colm was capable of overseeing this task. Then, Pogo had died. The other events hurt him because of his shortcomings as a son and the weakness of his body and its pain threshold. Pogo's death was straightforwardly painful, uncomplicated and free of contradictory emotions. There was no cynicism, no bitterness. He loved Pogo and felt his loss acutely and earnestly.

In hindsight, he'd become complacent in his self-pity. He lay awake until four, sometimes five in the morning, before finally drifting off to sleep. When his alarm went off a couple of hours later, getting out of bed felt impossible. He found himself running late by ten, twenty, thirty minutes. He wore whatever shirt was lying on the box-room floor, often the same one three days in a row, and he regularly found himself halfway to work before realising he hadn't brushed his teeth. He slammed his fist against the steering wheel and cursed. He started talking to himself like a child: It's ridiculous! A simple daily task and still you can't even manage that. He would worry all day about the smell of his breath when dealing with customers and other staff. And really, if a person was that negligent with their teeth, things that take two minutes to clean, didn't they deserve to feel rotten about their personal hygiene all day? His self-reproach during the drive to work was often so harsh that he took satisfaction from it; it was like scratching at an insect bite.

The late start also meant Colm missed out on the limited staff parking and was forced to use the customer car park, which was busy and cramped. It angered him to see how many people drove to work when he knew for a fact that, unlike him, most of them lived within walking distance.

This morning, he rushed out of his car, walking along the gravel towards the credit union he'd worked in for fourteen years. He hadn't noticed the car reversing from where it was parked – he was plucking tiny balls of fluff from the leg and crotch of his trousers. He could do it all day and they'd still look too shabby. Everything looked worse in the light of day. As he collided with the boot of the car, it came to an abrupt halt. It had struck his hip and shoulder. He didn't fall over but he did have to stumble backwards slightly to stay upright. It was almost painless. Mostly, he was embarrassed – it wouldn't have happened had he just left on time. His colleagues probably witnessed his clumsiness through the window, and even if they felt sorry for him, the sympathy would be unpleasant because they'd also wonder why he couldn't just get to work on time. It had been said to him more than once that a little organisation on his part would solve a lot of his problems.

In his frustration at these imagined judgements, he slammed a palm against the tail-light of the reversing car, which was at the same height as his shoulder. The fact that the car was a huge SUV, a monstrous-looking thing, something he considered totally unsuitable for a residential area, only served to enrich his anger. He rushed on then, suddenly aware of his fleeting rage and the possible implications. The car pulled out and crawled alongside him before stopping. He averted his eyes but in his peripheral vision he saw the tinted windows rolling down, slowly.

'Did you just *slam* your hand against my car?' the driver asked incredulously, sliding her sunglasses up from her eyes and over her hair. She was blonde and appeared athletic. She wore a purple cotton jumper and a black gilet. He noticed her jaw was a little too large for her face, her lips a little too puffy. 'How *dare* you? Don't walk away from me, I'm talking to you.'

At this Colm scoffed and rolled his eyes as if exasperated, although he was trembling. 'Listen, if you hadn't been reversing so fast, you wouldn't have bumped into me.' He carried on walking, but she continued to drive on alongside him.

'D'you *work* here? You do, don't you?' She had a northside accent that he suspected she was exaggerating, which irritated him. The question irritated him too, as it was clearly a threat. She saw this man, with his crumpled shirt and his tousled hair, and thought, Yeah, of course I can reverse over him with my ridiculous car and still claim to be the person most inconvenienced by the situation.

'Look,' he reasoned, forgetting he was late to work. 'Why are *you* so upset? I'm the pedestrian here. *I'm* the one who would have been injured if I *hadn't* slammed my hand against that hideous car you're driving.' He poked himself in the chest. 'I took a *preventive* measure, to protect myself. If I hadn't, I'm the one who would have been worse off. Not you and not your ugly car.'

'You weren't paying attention,' she persisted. 'You weren't watching where you were walking and you got aggressive with my car. You could have caused an accident and now, when I point that out to you, you continue to be aggressive.'

'Aggressive? Are you joking? I had right of way, I'm the pedestrian, the victim, in this hypothetical accident that you're blaming on me.' He gestured to her car. 'You're the one looming over me, in a monster truck, and you feel *threatened*? I have brittle bones!' This was a lie that came to him fluently and unexpectedly. Apart from the slipped disc, his bones were fine. He pressed on, regardless. 'You could have rolled right over me without even realising.'

She pointed out the window at him. 'I'm a customer here and I'd be very careful if I were you. I know the *board members* for this credit union. In fact, I know the director of the board, who happens to be a close relative of mine.'

For the first time in this interaction, he hesitated. He knew the director, a stern man who had always made Colm feel as though he were hiding something. Could this tacky woman be related to him? The car rolled slowly beside him. The driver of the car behind her grew impatient and beeped, but he felt only vaguely aware of this. Colm approached the woman's side window and saw, in his peripheral vision, his reflection in the shiny car door. It had distorted his image so that he looked shorter and squatter than he was, which made him inexplicably sad and even more frustrated.

As he placed his hand on the car door, he looked up into the window and watched her rear back slightly, the seatbelt straining against her collarbone. Her skin was orange and very sun damaged, covered in light-coloured freckles. She had very white teeth, but the interstitial spaces were brown and solid looking, as if she'd bleached the surface but, like Colm, didn't bother to floss. There were several empty water bottles strewn across the passenger seat and car floor, as well as a partially peeled half-eaten banana.

In the fleeting moment before he spoke again, he felt certain that she was careless with all her possessions, her teeth, her car. Her house was probably filled with expensive furniture that she didn't know how to take care of. She probably took dozens of flights a year, with no regard for the consequences. He was certain she didn't recycle, that she bought cheap new clothes made by poor labourers in Pakistan every other week. Did she have any idea how toxic her behaviour was? He'd bet she threw everything away as soon as it showed signs of disrepair, that she had no respect for history or culture. What a waste! He'd bet her entire home and life was a disorganised pigsty.

He leaned in towards her, speaking in a low hiss, his teeth gritted: 'Do you have any idea what you're doing to the environment, driving around in this thing? Do you care, *at all*, about the damage you're doing? Are you that ignorant, that you just don't care?'

She jabbed at a button and the window started to roll up against his face. She began to accelerate but he followed alongside her. She sped up and he was left trailing behind, jogging behind her car. Am I chasing her? he asked himself. Yes, I am, he realised, I'm chasing her as she drives away in her car, pumping my arms like the Terminator.

Her car slowed at the stop sign at the exit of the car park. His body slammed against the boot, and he gave the rear tyre a weak kick before hurrying around to her window.

'You don't live in the Rocky Mountains, you know. This is Dublin! We have cycleways and accessible public transport,' he shouted through the glass.

His voice was wheedling, and it almost reminded him of Norma, as he shouted, '*Shame* on you!' through the rolled-up glass of her car window. When she finally tore down the road away from him, he felt compelled to carry on chasing her, to relentlessly pursue her all the way home. He actually *wanted* to frighten her, he realised.

The thing that stopped him was the credit union manager, Dominic, striding across the car park towards him, his face grave, followed by Margaret, one of the tellers. Her plump hands were pressed against her mouth, and she was stumbling in her little heels. This was the same woman whom he'd shared a drunken kiss with at the Christmas party twelve years earlier, who claimed she had forgotten all about it when he tried to apologise afterwards. Their previous flirtation had been replaced with cold courtesy, and they found themselves suddenly pretending not to know each other very well. The fact that it was Margaret who'd witnessed the frail tail-end of his rage, someone who had rubbed her hips frantically against his, and not one of the newer, younger tellers who already spoke to him like a cute but elderly dog, felt disproportionately unfortunate.

He noticed Margaret hesitate before placing a hand on his shoulder. Momentarily, he empathised with her. It was difficult to comfort a person in this situation, while trying to avoid the fact that you had once been attracted to one another. But still, he recoiled from her touch, shaking her off and resenting her pity, her reserved surprise that some-one as harmless as Colm could have such an outburst.

'Colm,' she said, weakly, reaching toward his face.

The day was getting warmer, too warm for this time in the morning, and the sunlight felt overbearing on Colm's scalp. His heart was racing and he was breathless. He placed his hands on his hips and strode around in circles, taking in noisy gulps of air. Shortly after the woman drove away, Colm's outrage evaporated. In its place was the knowledge that he wasn't the kind of person who could get away with this sort of thing, he just wasn't. He had hoped to brush it all off, to reassure Dominic and Marga-ret that he was neither at fault nor too badly damaged after the incident. Instead, he heard coming from his own mouth a gradual rambling, a convoluted line of enquiry, directed at no one in particular. What was it about him that made people think he could be walked all over? Why couldn't people just be decent to each other? He was a *good* person, he insisted, a good *man*, who, you know what, deserved respect, at the very least, didn't he deserve respect? All the while, Dominic walked beside him, like a boxer's manager, his hand placed gently between Colm's shoulder blades.

*

It was Norma who was summoned to retrieve him. She had been playing badminton in the community hall, a short walk away. He watched her stride alongside the moss-covered brick wall lining the credit union, dressed in baggy shorts and a pink t-shirt that had 'Miami' printed across the chest. She was red in the face and perspiring. She looked puzzled by his dishevelled appearance – he had only left the house an hour ago – and seemed to hesitate in approaching him. Colm walked to meet her in the middle of the car park, his legs stiff, and dropped his car keys into her hand. Without saying goodbye to Dominic, he walked to his car, opened the passenger door and climbed in. He took a deep breath, through closed teeth. He could smell his own body odour. His rumpled shirt was soaked in a cold sweat, the kind that reminded him of having his teeth drilled at the dentist. In the rearview mirror, he could see Norma talking to Dominic and Margaret. She looked bewildered and apologetic. Colm placed a hand over his eyes.

As soon as she sat in the car, he asked her to start driving. He couldn't stand that Dominic stayed watching him at the entrance to the credit union, waiting for the car to pull out, as though wanting to make sure they left the premises.

The drive home was almost silent, and Colm was grateful of how little traffic they encountered. After a short journey, they reached the large estate where their house was situated, near the back, close to the football pitch. They'd bought it because it had such an ample garden, ideal for children. Now, the garden was destroyed by their dog Joey and Colm was the only one who cleaned up the dog shit.

Norma parked Colm's car next to a small a Fiat Punto, the car they used to teach Francis to drive. Truthfully, he could practise only with Norma. Being instructed by Colm left his son frustrated and defeated. Norma turned off the ignition and turned to Colm, her eyes wide.

'When Dominic called me,' she began, quietly, 'I thought that you'd had a heart attack and dropped dead, or something.'

Colm only shook his head and raised a hand, signalling that he couldn't speak.

He noticed her chest and shoulders shudder slightly.

'Are you trying not to laugh?' he asked incredulously. Her eyes grew wide in innocent denial. 'I'm not stupid, I can tell you're trying not to laugh.'

She hid her mouth with her fingertips. 'I'm so sorry, it's just so strange. You're making me nervous.'

Colm got out of the car without responding, and walked to their front door. The house was empty, and immaculate, when they entered. He sank into his armchair in the sitting room and leaned his face into a hand.

'Wouldn't you like to get changed?' Norma asked, gently.

Colm only shook his head, without lifting his face.

She retreated from the sitting room, leaving him alone. It took less than an hour for Dominic to call the landline, speaking to Norma directly. Colm heard Norma say: 'Oh, Dominic, you know it's so unlike him. He's like a beaten dog in there, honestly.'

The conversation went on for several minutes, which made Colm feel nervous. How had he not considered there would be further consequences? After Norma hung up the phone, she waited a while before joining him in the sitting room. In the meantime, Colm wondered if he'd be sacked. Although he had a hard time getting out of bed in the mornings, he wasn't sure he could cope without his job. He wasn't even thinking of the financial consequences: it was the idea of being home with Norma all day, being criticised and hassled and made to feel like a nuisance and a burden. He could imagine how little she'd enjoy his constant presence. The sitting-room door opened, and Norma crossed the threshold. She had showered and was now wearing a white blouse and a pair of linen trousers.

'Well, my, my, my,' was all she said at first.

Perhaps she had hoped to convey regret or sympathy, but all Colm heard was her self-righteousness. A memory resurfaced, from years ago. The short spell she did in hospital, after Francis was born, leaving Colm to manage everything. When she'd come home, she hadn't appeared grateful or relieved that he'd kept the show on the road in her absence. She'd just seemed disappointed that the house was in such disarray. He hadn't held any of it against her, hadn't thrown it in her face. He liked to think this was due to compassion, but, if he was honest, there was an under-lying spite to his refusal to admit he felt hard done by. His reticence allowed the resentment to deepen in colour and viscosity. Even now, the longer he tolerated her con-tempt for him, the better he thought he was as a person. With every dismissive remark he ignored, it was like slip-ping a coin into a piggy bank. It was nice to see things accumulate.

He was acting like his own mother, he knew that. It was a behaviour his father had identified in Colm and discour-aged, cautioning him of the bitterness, the martyrdom. Colm had been stunned by the accuracy of this observa-tion and despised his father, briefly, for knowing his private thoughts. He hated that his motives were the same as those of a middle-aged woman – it was humiliating. But the bit-terness was compelling, the private feeling of superiority refreshing for a person who outwardly presented as humble and easy-going. Now, the overflow had got the better of him and the scales had tipped, the years of his quiet suffering squandered.

Colm looked at her now, in the sitting room, through splayed fingers.

'You're not so perfect yourself,' he said.

Norma froze, perplexed, and peered at him as if he were drunk. She pressed on, hesitantly. 'That woman, in the car, called in to make a complaint. She said you assaulted her.'

'Right,' he said, his voice strangled and strange.

'Apparently she's Richard's niece, the chairman, which is bad luck.' Norma lowered herself onto the arm of the couch.

Colm shrugged and looked up at her. 'What do you think Dominic will do?' he asked.

'Disciplinary hearing and leave of absence,' Norma said. 'Dominic told me that Richard likes you and that anyway, he thinks this niece of his is fond of causing trouble. He suspects that there was two of you in it.

'He did wonder if you might benefit from speaking to someone about how you're feeling,' she continued. 'Given that it's been such a difficult time for you.'

'Well, of course it's been a difficult time for me,' Colm cried in frustration. 'I'm not even wanted in my own home, by my own family.'

Norma raised her eyebrows, but didn't say anything.

'Neither you nor Francis have any interest in what I think, or what I have to say. I do my best to understand the two of you, to help you, but it's obvious you don't care what I think.'

'For God's sake, Colm,' she began, her voice wavering with suppressed amusement.

'No,' Colm snapped, pointing a finger at her. 'It's true and it's very lonely for me.'

At this, Norma appeared to soften. 'Come on now, it's not that we don't want you around, not at all. It's just, you never seem all that interested in what either of us has to say,' she ventured cautiously. 'And to be quite honest, sometimes it feels to me that you think you're better than your family, that we're too ignorant or shallow for you.

But it doesn't mean we don't *love* you. We just have a difficult time relating to each other, sometimes. Lots of families
have that problem.' She glanced at him surreptitiously as
she spoke.

Her response was so reasonable, so sensible, that it hurt
him to hear it. It made him sad for both of them and he
wished he hadn't said anything. Now she knew about his
resentment, a thing that struck him as childish and self-
pitying. He couldn't take it back either, because he sensed
that she had already known: all they had done was acknowledge it.

'In what way do you think that I believe I'm *better* than
you and Francis?' he asked.

'Well,' she began, her voice suddenly wobbling, 'sometimes I'll tell you a story about something that happened
or something I'm interested in, and you have this habit of
taking a deep breath, as if bracing yourself for having to
listen to me, as if you don't really believe me or care what
I'm saying. It's *hurtful*.'

'Ah, come on, no, I *don't*. You can't know what I'm
thinking by how I'm breathing,' Colm said, reflexively.

'You actually did it right before I started speaking earlier. Sometimes you roll your eyes too.' She paused then,
appearing pensive. 'Remember we went for dinner, a
couple of weeks ago with your brothers? You did it then,
when I couldn't pronounce the meal that I was ordering.'
She looked at him directly. 'I feel afraid to speak up around
your family, to tell a story or talk at length, because I can
feel you watching me, willing me to shut up. I often think
you're ashamed of me.'

Colm was stunned. The information winded him. She was right – he did do that. He had just assumed he was too covert to be noticed. He'd overestimated himself.

'I admit that maybe I do try to exclude you,' Norma shrugged, 'because of your behaviour. I don't mean to make life difficult for you. I have my reasons, but I can see how it could be unpleasant.'

'Right,' he said, taking a deep breath. Then: 'Oh, that wasn't me bracing myself or anything, just processing.'

Her lips were pressed together and drawn out thin. She nodded.

It wasn't even noon, and the day was full of surprises. Norma, in her spotless, pressed linen trousers, crossed the room and knelt on the floor, so that they were almost face to face. Sunlight fell diagonally across half the room. With one hand she clasped his and with the other patted his knee. It reminded him of the days before and after his father's funeral. He'd been at home all week and the time had stretched out, patiently. There had been many people coming and going, and it had surprised him how much he appreciated this. Maybe he was naive, but it had given him a sense of community. Norma had played an important part during this time and they'd been uncharacteristically gentle with one another. It was like they had been part of the same organism, an extension of all the other people around them too. The procession of friends and family coming and going seemed to disturb the earlier agitation and tension between them, so that it constantly swirled overhead like dust, never having a chance to settle and take hold.

Colm had wondered why he had ever wanted to be alone, why he allowed friendships to fade. The feeling of community had lasted another four or five days. It even lingered bravely for a day after everyone drifted away. He'd been afraid he was too frail for normality but it had returned regardless. Now, it was just Colm and Norma, and he could feel it again. It takes a crisis, he guessed. He heard Francis arrive home and sneeze three times in the kitchen. Joey barked at the breeze in the garden. Colm felt a familiar urge to resist Norma's support, out of spite, but he thought it wise to ignore this instinct and instead see what would happen if he sat there for another minute, then two, letting her hold his hand.

*

Later in the day, they had the television on. It was a daytime game show, a rerun from years ago. The contestants' clothes appeared dated and strange now. He felt drowsy in his chair.

'You should let yourself go to sleep, Colm,' Norma said, gently. It wouldn't last, this kindness between them, it was a temporary thing, but that didn't mean it wasn't important. Maybe, he thought, it would keep happening like this. Tomorrow they could lose this tender feeling, and it might not return to them for years. Maybe that was just the way it was supposed to be for them.

'If I sleep now, I won't sleep later,' he replied. His eyes felt heavy.

'That doesn't matter, you won't sleep tonight anyway,' she said quietly.

She was right — he wouldn't sleep at night no matter what he did. He heard Norma ask him a rambling, confusing question. Was this the same show where the host's wife was a producer but then he *left* his wife for one of the contestants? Or was this the show where the host married one of the contestants, therefore innocent of any infidelity? Colm didn't know and he didn't answer her. His eyes had already closed, and soon he had drifted off entirely.

Removal

I worry so much about the weather in Alberta. If it continues to snow, I won't get enough hours at work. I need to get this tooth out but I don't have the money. The dentist keeps me waiting in the chair. I hear him walking back and forth behind the curtain, talking on the phone, complaining about his taxes. There's a problem with the price of oil and it's ruined everything. When he gets around to examining me, he says, Yes, it's an infected wisdom tooth. He'll give me an antibiotic, as a short-term fix.

'But you've already got too many teeth,' he warns. 'They're too big and your mouth is too small.'

He's digging intently at my molars with a pointed metal instrument, nodding his head forwards as he pulls and yanks.

'That's *why* they're so crooked, see,' he adds, then, quietly.

The dentist snaps off his rubber gloves, spins away from me in his chair and starts typing up a prescription.

'How much will it cost?' I ask.

He grimaces. 'Does your job offer dental insurance?'

I shake my head no. 'I work in a restaurant, for now, but it closes after Christmas until the summer.'

'Yeah,' he says absently, 'it's tough for everybody right now. For one thing, taxes are so high here, what can you do?' He taps the last few keys and stands to pull the curtain aside for me. 'I don't discuss payment with patients. You can do that with the girls out front.'

The examination costs one hundred and ten dollars and the antibiotic costs twenty. It's going to cost me about five hundred to get the tooth out, so every time it starts to throb, I'll just have to sit very still and wait for it to pass.

*

I'm working the door with the other host, Charlene. It's a Christmas party for an oil-extraction company. The restaurant is boat-themed, the furniture made out of beat-up, broken-down canoes, and there are models of whole fish mounted on the walls. All I'm allowed to do is take coats and pour water. A few years ago, I'd have resented such limited responsibility, as if I was too smart for it. Now, I've adjusted to this kind of work. I've been doing it, in different places, for ten years. I find myself nervous when I'm asked to carry a glass of wine or write the specials on the chalkboard. Often, I forget to grip the stem, or I have to rewrite the specials over and over because my handwriting is too small and crooked.

Unlike me, Charlene is a local girl. She's lived here all her life. We're both tall and blonde, but she has a better face. She wears plain and subtly sophisticated clothes. I try to recreate her block colours and manly brogues, but I end up looking religious. The oil men flirt with Charlene as they lay their heavy winter coats into our open arms. They mostly ignore me and because of this, I give them nothing but bland smiles. When I have to look at one of them, I focus on whatever is slightly above their heads.

For each person who drops off a coat, we give them a number tag and then put a corresponding number tag on their coat. Except I'm getting mixed up because they're all rushing by so quickly, half of them aren't even taking the tag. 'This one was number seventeen,' Charlene says, trying to help. 'This one was twenty-two.' Then she dumps her own pile in my arms before turning to greet the new arrivals.

I hurry off to the cloak room. Some of the coats slip from my arms and trail along the floor. Charlene watches me and shakes her head despairingly.

There are a lot of wives here too. I circle around the first table, offering still or sparkling, again and again, like I'm rehearsing my one line in a play. I lean in to adjust the position of one lady's glass and she cranes her neck up to scowl at me. She's old and her face is trembling.

'You touched the rim of my glass,' she complains, tapping it with a crooked finger. 'It's smudged. That happens to be where I put my *mouth*, you know.'

Her voice is weak and the room is echoing with chatter. No one else has heard her, so I just tilt my face in an expression of pleasant interest, as if she has told me about an accomplished grandchild or a recent trip to Europe. Her mouth gapes momentarily and she touches her husband's wrist. He's turned away from her, speaking to another woman. I cross the table, moving on before she can repeat herself.

As I walk away, I see that John the bartender has been watching me, smirking. He is Charlene's boyfriend. He's a twenty-year-old who came here for the summer and decided to stick around. So far, after six months here, he is my closest friend. He probably wouldn't spend time with me if he weren't an outsider too. I'm sure in his real life, he wouldn't have any reason to be friends with a woman almost ten years older than he is. I'm sure he wouldn't spend his Friday nights sitting on my bunk bed at the cheap university accommodation I rent, where I am also the only person who isn't in college.

Mostly, it's innocent. All we ever do is kiss and hold hands while watching movies on my laptop. I like to play movies he hasn't seen before, like *An American Werewolf in London* or *Full Metal Jacket*, just to see his reaction. I always pick, he never has any good ideas. I only want to kiss him, nothing more than that. It's not just that I know he's already having sex with Charlene. He is so beautiful to me that to do anything other than kiss would feel like a violation. I never imagined being with someone this physically attractive. It's not something I had ever experienced before, and I know that he is beautiful in a way that I am not. But isn't it true that I had imagined life might start once I came here? So much of it is going wrong: where I live, the money, sneaking around. I'd imagined romance – not like this, but this is how it's happening, this is the way I am living.

He can be immature though, a little too dramatic. He says he has a sick sister whom he sends money to every week but

I don't believe him — he works even less than I do. The sister's disease is chronic but vague, her diagnoses changing and accumulating. He says it's a private burden, that I can't tell anyone, but every time I turn a corner at work, I see him with his head hung low, sadly explaining his situation to anyone who will listen. That's one thing I don't like about him: he lacks discretion and I can tell he rehearses his stories.

At the end of October, we have an argument on the train. A homeless man in a thin shirt with missing buttons approaches and asks if he can sing to us. John ignores him. I smile politely and shake my head. The man lingers, offended by our disinterest. I give him twenty dollars, the tip money from my shift earlier that day.

'It's okay, you don't need to sing,' I smile at him.

He accepts the money, but it doesn't help; we have still hurt his feelings by refusing his services. He turns away, his face glum.

When we get off the train, John scolds me for giving away money I don't have. 'You're poor too,' he says.

'I'm not poor,' I say.

'You should be saving your money. It's stupid to be generous when you can't afford to.'

'Well, you give away your money,' I shrug.

'That's different. That's family. And I have another job lined up. You haven't even been looking for work,' he says.

'Yes, I have,' I insist. 'All the restaurants are closing.'

He is quiet for a moment.

'Why don't you apply for something else, something a little more permanent?' he asks. 'Office work, a receptionist job.'

'I *have*,' I say quietly.

I don't tell him that I've submitted my CV to a recruitment agency, but most places want someone with more experience.

'It's just, you're old enough to want something a little more reliable,' he says. 'I look at some of the servers at work who are older than you and it looks tough, they look tired. It's not always easy going on welfare for the whole winter.'

'I'm not going on welfare,' I snap. 'I can't anyway, I don't have that kind of visa.'

'Well, someone will give you a chance. It's better to have a degree but you could just lie. You're not from here, they won't know,' he says, cheerfully, trying to turn things around.

I sigh and look at my feet, wet with snow. I regret telling him that I left college in my second year. I couldn't cope with the theory and the rhetoric. I was numb with stupidity. I've had lots of jobs since, in barbershops and off-licences and supermarkets and hotels, but it's just been a series of side-steps for the last ten years. I had planned for better opportunities here. I could do administrative work or be a receptionist. I'm not afraid of hard work, I'm eager to explain. But it doesn't look good, to have had so many jobs, none of them for more than a year, with all those little gaps, so no one is calling me back.

John usually spends his weekends with Charlene. The weather's too cold for walking – my hair turns white if I'm out there for more than a minute, so I'm often bored if I'm not working. People warned me of the cold before coming here, but I suspected they were exaggerating. Possibly, I also incorrectly categorised myself as intrepid and immune to harsh conditions. If you told me last year that I'd spend much of my free time dithering over whether I should or shouldn't masturbate when I really ought to be doing something more productive, I wouldn't have moved here. Although, I probably wouldn't have believed that this was what lay ahead in the first place.

On my days off, I usually end up calling my mother. We talk for a full hour sometimes, unless her husband is there, in which case she's cheerful and vague, as if she's being held hostage. When I call her at the end of November, she's alone. She is enduring her latest period of sobriety, the third month of it after crashing her car in September. The last time I was at her house, I found dozens of empty cough-syrup bottles in the hot press, lined up between the towels. It's always something, with her.

She asks me about the job situation and I am honest with her, pacing the carpet of my room.

'You'll be okay. You're like me, clever. And you're not afraid to do the work no one else wants to,' she says, surprising me.

I feel like saying that we're not clever, look at our lives. I feel like saying horrible things about myself, just to hurt her, to make her feel like she has failed. I don't though, because we're too far away from each other to be having those old fights again. Now, we have no way of getting to each other, so that we can apologise and cry into each other's necks. I have to be able to live with what I say to her, from this distance.

*

'We have a problem,' John tells me in the middle of December. 'Charlene's friend lives in the same building as you. She's seen us together, a *lot*. She told me that if I don't tell Charlene what's going on, she will.'

I'm sitting on the bed. He's leaning against the windowsill.

'I'm going to have to tell her,' he says, shaking his head.

'Why would you do that?' I object. 'There's nothing to show we've done anything wrong.'

'Come on, she's not stupid,' he says impatiently. 'Why else would we hang out?'

'We'll just say that we're friends,' I insist.

'Why would we be friends?' he asks.

'I don't know, actually,' I shrug. It hurts me, but it is an honest question. It doesn't seem to dawn on him that I might find this upsetting.

'Just out of curiosity,' I begin, 'if you had to choose between us, would you ever choose me?'

I do not look at him as he answers. I focus on a spot right above his head, a patch of dense, grey cloud visible through the window.

Later that week, I am back in work, doing a dinner shift. John has agreed to wait until the restaurant closes before he talks to Charlene, so I am not especially uneasy. It's a slow night, so I spend most of my time in the back, by the stairwell, polishing cutlery. I'm dipping the silverware into chrome buckets filled with hot water, and wiping it off with a napkin. I hear someone approach, their footfall quick and heavy. Charlene stands very close to me. She grips the edge of the bucket with one hand and places the other on her hip. She exhales noisily and presses her lips together. I realise with a start that she already knows. I care more than I had expected to.

'Charlene—'

She cuts me off by rattling the bucket of cutlery, hard. It doesn't topple but some water slops over the edge.

'Find your *own* fucking boyfriend,' she hisses quietly.

Later, I call John. 'Well, thanks for waiting,' I say.

'It wasn't me, I promise' he insists. He sounds defeated and anxious. I can't help but feel sorry for him. I know how it feels, to be that age, to have pushed a door you should have pulled. 'Her friend went and told her anyway,' he says, 'even though she said she wouldn't.'

My last shift is New Year's Eve. Charlene no longer works here. It turns out she found a new job even before she found out about me and John. The other girls here ignore me out of loyalty to Charlene. They rarely spoke to me anyway, so the fact that I feel so hurt and self-conscious is a surprise. The atmosphere is festive, the people growing noisier, more expressive, the more they drink. There's a staff party scheduled for later on, once all the customers leave. My manager has invited me but no one else has mentioned it. It's supposed to be a celebration, a reward for our hard work this season, but the idea of a party makes me feel lonely, especially because I know that, after tonight, I won't have a job. I won't even see John, who has been avoiding me.

There are other women in my job whom I could have

made friends with. I could have integrated myself into their lives, joined them for weekend hikes. I snubbed them, making sweeping assumptions based on petty assessments. They talked a lot about lip fillers and eyelash extensions so I judged them to be the kind of women who got sucked into pyramid schemes and didn't believe in reproductive rights. These were stories I had made up in my own mind, without any proof. I silently mocked them while eavesdropping on their earnest expressions of desire for a better life, one in which they made more money and had the kind of partner who shared their dreams and saw their value. I mocked them, in my own mind and to John and my mother, and then convinced myself that they were the ones to snub me.

At almost nine o'clock, I hear the heavy front door swing open and slam shut. I turn to see a man wavering on his feet, clearly drunk. He looks to be in his seventies, but his hair is long and dyed blonde. As he approaches, I can tell he isn't about to order any food. Still, I offer him a menu. He laughs at my extended hand and then seems disappointed that I'm frightened. He's wearing a bomber-style jacket zipped up to his sternum with no shirt underneath it. His bare chest is orange, and I imagine he must use sun beds to achieve this colour. I can tell he was muscular, up until a point. His skin appears thick, like his organs are buried a foot deep inside.

After a moment or two, I realise it's not his deflated form that makes me sad but the fact that he's wearing women's reading glasses. They're the cheap ones that are sold in pharmacies beside hair clips and nail scissors. My mother owns several pairs. I find myself wondering if he simply could not afford a visit to the optician, or if he just liked the look of the purple-framed ones he's now wearing and decided to treat himself. It is the latter possibility that stirs in me a tender feeling. My eyes linger on his frostbitten hands that are missing several fingers, and he notices that I'm staring. I avert my gaze, trying to redirect us to the appropriate course of action. I ask would he like to sit at the bar or at a table, again sensing that there is something unpredictable and uncooperative happening between us. He sneers at me like he can see every dirty, cruel thing I've ever done in my life, like he recognises my pity as being false and condescending. I don't want anything to do with him, and he knows it.

He turns away from me and looks around, clutching his belt buckle. Diners bristle as he walks past them on his way to the bar. My manager approaches him and asks if he'd like something to eat. She doesn't want him here but speaks to him as though she'd love nothing more than for him to stay. He tells her he has no money and she offers bread and coffee, instead. He doesn't like this and asks for a drink, louder this time. My manager says she cannot give him the drink and suggests he go home to have a rest. He pushes past her in a temper, and on his way out deliberately and swiftly tips over a diner's bowl of split pea and sausage soup. The diner holds his spoon mid-air and stares at the green liquid and chunks of meat splattered across his lap in disgust.

*

By the end of January, it has been four weeks since I've gotten a payslip. I thought I'd be able to stretch things out, but I was wrong. I am so broke that all I can afford are tomatoes and bread. I'm flushing my mouth with salt water every night to ward off a chronic but low-level tooth infection. My mother worries I will get sepsis. I send her a text, asking if she could loan me money to get the tooth out. She replies immediately, asking if I can wait another two weeks. She includes in her text a list of her own bills and her current funds. She also follows up with a text to say it is a shame that it hasn't panned out for me as I had hoped. I can picture her saying this to her husband, telling him that I've always been this way, allowing money to fall between my fingers. I want to reply and say, Tell me again how we're clever. Tell me again how we're hard-working. What about us would suggest these qualities?

In the first week of February, I cut through the park to get home from the supermarket, carrying a paper bag containing tomatoes, bread, eggs and off-brand Corsodyl. Over by the pond, I see the man from the restaurant. I recognise him immediately, from his hair and his build. He is stumbling along the water's edge. An elderly couple pass by and he trails along after them, probably asking for money. When they ignore him, he clutches at his jacket and doubles over, in anguish. The fact that he is completely silent while doing so makes it appear more dramatic. He stumbles forwards again, still bent over like that.

I observe him briefly before moving on, I don't want him to notice me. I'm embarrassed to remember back to October, when I had money to give to the homeless man on the train, the one who wanted to sing for me. John had been right: it was irresponsible, giving it away like that. I do let money slip through my fingers — it was easier and cheaper to give it away for nothing than to say, No, I don't want to hear you sing. I'd prefer to be stumbling through dull and poorly paid jobs than feel the inadequacy and stupidity that might come from pursuing a stable, promising career that most people can do without it proving too difficult. Anything to avoid humiliation, however minor, or conditions that might require resilience. I still hope that I'll see John again, even though he doesn't want to be with me, not in the way I want him to. And I'd rather avoid the frightening man in the park in case he tries to talk to me, not because I find him revolting but because how can I say no to him? I'd end up pretending that I'd love to chat, to walk together, only to cruelly slip away once he'd turned his back to point to the geese or tie his shoe laces, just as he'd started to feel like I reminded him of someone else.

That night, I wake up with a shooting pain in my jaw. When I go to the bathroom to rinse my mouth with salt water, I look in the mirror and see that my face is swollen and purple, as if I am concealing a golf ball between my cheek and teeth. My mouth is too painful to pry open and look inside; the salt water dribbles back out, down the sink.

I try to lie back down and go to sleep but now that I'm awake, the throbbing is relentless and I'm frightened by the swelling. I know I need to go to the hospital; the pain is too urgent. This isn't the problem though. While dental care is still expensive, Canadian hospital visits are free.

The problem is the snow: it's heavy and I can hardly see out my window. It's not far, but I'm not sure I could stand the cold for longer than a few minutes. I decide to call John, the only person I know well enough to ask for help at three in the morning. I message first, to ask if he's awake. After ten minutes, he has not responded so I call him. It rings out. A taxi will cost me between fifteen and twenty dollars and I'll probably end up needing to buy some medicine and how much will that cost? Despite knowing this is not money I can afford to spend, I decide there's nothing I can do about it, so I order a taxi on my phone. Within twenty minutes, I am at the emergency department.

The wait time is less than an hour and the receptionist and triage nurse are both pleasant and efficient. Their cheerful sympathy has a calming effect and even though my mouth still throbs, the pain is bearable in this environment. The nurse, who looks younger than me, leaves me to wait in a small room on a bed covered by a paper sheet. Shortly after, the doctor arrives. I had expected someone tired and disinterested but he is kind and patient, squeezing my ankle to reassure me.

After peering inside my mouth, he tells me the tooth is impacted and badly infected. 'How long have you had this problem?' he asks.

'Since late September, on and off, I think.' Even as I say it, I feel a rush of shame that I have not managed to get it removed in all this time.

'September?' he repeats incredulously.

Noticing my embarrassment, he squeezes my ankle

once more. 'It's okay, I'm not scolding you, I'm just amazed we're only seeing you now. You have to be very careful with dental problems, particularly impacted teeth,' he explains, waving a hand around his face. 'People only think about teeth when they want a pretty smile. But if you had left this any longer and the infection spread, you could have ended up with a brain injury.

'But you're here now,' he continues, 'and we can give you some strong antibiotics, some steroids and some codeine. But be careful with the codeine. Only take that when you need it.'

I nod. 'And what about the tooth?' I ask. 'Can you take it out?'

He shakes his head. 'No, it's too infected. You'll have to wait until it's healed. Even then, you will need a dental surgeon.'

I am home a little after six in the morning. My phone died on the way back and when I charge it, I see two messages arrive from John. The first says he didn't see my calls or texts, that he was asleep. The second is a longer message, telling me that he doesn't think we should be in contact anymore, that we can't be friends because he's trying to make it work with Charlene. He wishes me a lot of luck and hopes that I understand. I don't even finish the message, I put down my phone. He watches too much TV, I say to myself, thinks everything is a big deal. But even after I nap and take some codeine, the messages still bother me, like little stones in my shoe.

*

In late February, I get a receptionist job at a recruitment agency, of all places. They have no problem telling me that my predecessor left because she couldn't handle the bull pen. I think they must have no lives outside the office, if this is how they talk. They need me to start right away and I do. I fill out the employee forms carefully and triple check my bank details. By the time they pay me, I have eight dollars and thirty-two cents left.

The young female recruiters ignore me. They are cruel to prospective candidates who don't measure up. As soon as they're finished on the phone, they start talking about how desperate the candidates are, how unskilled. The young men aren't burdened with the same insecurities. The older men lean over my desk to chat, but don't invite me to lunch or after-work drinks because that type of thing isn't allowed any more. Sometimes they say inappropriate things. I know I'm not supposed to feel sorry for them but I do, because all these new rules must be confusing.

In March, I finally get the tooth out. In the meantime, I got another infection, but it was not so bad this time: I got by with the rest of the codeine from the hospital. The removal costs me five hundred dollars, which is still a lot of money to me. But it doesn't break me: I can still afford groceries and I only have to take three days off work. I go back to the same dentist I went to in September and he still complains about his taxes, while he yanks the rotten tooth out of my head. Afterwards, I feel superstitious about throwing it away, as though keeping it close to my body might ward off future adversity and pain. I ask him can I keep it, but when he shows it to me, it is tiny and grey, and when he squeezes it, it crumbles between his fingers.

A few weeks later, I find a new place to live. It's a little more expensive but I can't keep living in the dormitories. I move into a ground-floor apartment, which I share with an Italian girl who doesn't speak a lot of English. We communicate through hand gestures and play Jenga together. Sometimes I think it's probably better that we can't have a real conversation because at least we can't be unkind to each other.

The weather improves in April and I buy a beautiful blue bicycle from an English woman who lives eight blocks away. She tells me it takes at least two years to get used to everything, that when she first arrived, she lived in a hostel for several months and had to work three restaurant jobs just to get enough hours. I try not to linger too long because I can see she has her children to get back to. It's the first bike that I've owned as an adult. In the advertisement, it cost one hundred and fifty dollars, but when I try to give her the money, she won't take more than ninety.

I won't be able to use it in the winter, but I like the idea of being a young woman who cycles through the city on a nice bike. I like to think about what the men who see me cycle might assume about the other parts of my life. It occurs to me that I might be lonely, but I don't consider it a priority. It's only when I'm two blocks away from the woman's house, cycling up the first steep hill, that I realise there are no gears: the bike is a single-speed, designed for leisurely cycles over flat land. I feel stupid and self-conscious and stand up to put all my weight on the pedals but it's hard, I'm very out of shape. At the top, I reach a group of old men hanging around outside a café, smoking. I am breathless and sweating from the climb and the new heat. As I roll by, I hear them laugh, clap and whistle behind me.

Acknowledgements

I would like to thank my wonderful agent Angelique Tran Van Sang for all her unwavering support, encouragement and reassurance. Thank you, Ange, for having faith in my writing, and for giving the book so much time and consideration. You are incredibly kind and generous and your belief in this collection was hugely impactful. I'd also like to thank my incredible editor Željka Marošević, who seemed to instantly recognise what I was trying to achieve with the stories, which was very affirming. At times, it felt as though she understood the collection better than I did. Thank you Željka, for your clarity and insight and patience – what a dream to work with you on this book. I'd also like to thank both teams at Jonathan Cape and at Felicity Bryan for their support and assistance throughout this process; it has been a pleasure.

Massive thanks to the rare gem that is Tom Morris, a writer whose stories I know are widely beloved. Tom has been endlessly generous with his time and resources. The book would not exist without him. I doubt I can repay this generosity, but I do hope to follow Tom's example and make other emerging writers feel supported and included where I can. Thank you so much Tom; you have been such an important part of my writing life.

I'd also like to thank the writer John Patrick McHugh for his constant encouragement and support in writing this book. JP has been instrumental to my progress as a writer. The first story in this collection, 'Push and Pull', first appeared in *Fallow Media* and it was JP who commissioned and edited this story. Thank you, JP, for always showing an interest in my work and making me feel like a real writer.

Thank you to everyone at the *Stinging Fly*, particularly Declan Meade, as well as Sally Rooney. Sally published my first story during her time as editor, and when I received her email accepting the story, I cried in the bathroom at work. Thank you, Declan, for endlessly supporting emerging writers. I cannot imagine the writing community in Ireland without the *Stinging Fly*. Thank you to the Arts Council of Ireland for providing me with financial support on two occasions while I was writing this book.

Thank you to my friends for loving me, and supporting me. Many of you are artists and you inspire me every time we meet, driving me forward in my own creative pursuits. Thank you, Brigid O'Dea, Kathleen McDermott, Stephen Lau and Eamon McGuinness. There is so much excitement in being around creative people, and because I admire each of you so much, your kindness, encouragement and interest is incredibly important to me.

Separately, I'd like to thank Stephen Lau, Sean Kenny and Tessa Dunphy for being the funniest people I know. I miss you all, and I wish we could live in the same city again because the memories of that time are some of my happiest.

Thank you so much to my oldest friends, who fill my heart every time we meet: Aisling McGuinness, Orla Craigie, Clare McGonagle, Cristín Kelly, Máire O'Shaughnessy, Emma Fitzpatrick and Melanie Kirwan. Your friendship means the world to me and I adore you all.

Thank you so much to Phil and Alice Ryan, and all the Ryan family. Thank you for your kindness and care, and for making me feel like a part of your family; it means so much.

I'd like to thank my Nan and late Nana, for being such good storytellers and proving that brevity isn't always the best approach. I'd like to also extend my gratitude to: Catherine and Claire Quillinan, Martina and John Graham, Declan and Angelina Ivory, and Colm Storey. Additional thanks to Claire Kilty, and all my colleagues for their kindness and support, and to Nicola Mitchell, Lucy Nolan and Carol Barrett for their friendship. Thank you to Jennifer Lau and the Lau family, as well as Sarah Murray for their encouragement.

Huge thanks to my sister, Alex, my best friend, and her wonderful partner Aaron and my beautiful and funny niece and goddaughter Emie. I would be totally lost without them.

Family comes in many forms and for that I'd also like to thank Ciara Tobin, for treating me like a sister and supporting me and Alex in every way she could. Thank you to her husband, Seán, and their beautiful sons, Hugh, Joey and Cian, my lovely godson.

Thank you also to Niamh McKenna and her family, for always being so thoughtful and kind. And a massive thank you to Chris and Rory Gallagher, who welcomed me into their home almost every day as I grew up.

Therapy has influenced me as a writer massively. I'd like to thank my wonderful therapist, Elaine Claffey, who helped me discover that art and therapy are interlinked, and can influence each other. Thank you also to my first counsellor, Padraig, who never turned me away when I couldn't afford a session.

Thank you to my parents, Mick and Aileen, who I hope will not read this book. They have taught me nearly everything I know about storytelling. They are both so funny and unique, and I have learned so much about curiosity and creativity and music from them. I believe that my mother should have been a writer, and I hope that some-day she will sit down and write some of her own stories.

All of my love and gratitude to Philly, always. I wrote this book to impress you (I'm only sort of joking). You are so creative and determined, and one of the hardest-working people I know. I'm so proud of you and I wanted to make you proud. Thank you for making me laugh, every day, and for your endless patience, support and kindness; it means the world to me.

Finally, thank you to everyone who reads *Free Therapy*. I am so grateful to you for your time, and I hope you enjoy the stories.

About the Author

Rebecca Ivory was born in 1993 and is a writer based in Dublin. Her short fiction has appeared in the *Stinging Fly*, *Banshee*, *Tangerine* and *Fallow Media*. In 2020, she was awarded a Literature Bursary from the Arts Council of Ireland. *Free Therapy* is her debut.